In Spite of It All
A Maidstone Novel

By Sven "Swede" Anderson with Marc Youngquist

Swamp Dog Hollow LLC
PO Box 85
Middlefield, CT 06455

Cover design by Geoff Bottone and Marc Youngquist.
Geraldine Gormley Senior Editor.
Geoff Bottone Editor and layout design.

Editing Staff, Marcia Youngquist, James M. Cavanaugh,
William Bridges, Jon Bottone, and Randall J. Raines.

Copyright © 2019

ISBN: 978-1-09-088978-2

Chapter 1

Danny came straight up out of bed letting out an animal-like sound. The explosion he heard in his dream was as real as the night he heard the shotgun blast. His roommate rolled out of his bed gasping for air and staring into the darkness where his bunky had just scared the shit out of him.

"Not again," shouted the roommate.

Danny tried to catch his breath and slow his heart rate down. After a few seconds, things began to return to normal.

"Sorry," said Danny. "The shit keeps creeping back, and I have no control of my nightmares. It just happens, and then I wake up."

Mike was looking through the darkness and reached for the light. When the switch was thrown, he could clearly see that Danny was dripping wet and his chest was heaving. "Dude, you have got to go see someone about these dreams. This is the fourth time you have scared the shit out of me, and I don't scare easy. I did my time overseas. Once in a while I have my dreams but not every damn night and not with the intensity like you have. Don't take this the wrong way, but in the morning, I am going to get another room. I can't take this, and you need help."

All Danny could manage was, "Sorry."

Mike thought this was all about Iraq and Afghanistan. No one in the class had heard about the attempted murder in

Maidstone, Massachusetts. Danny had his share of close calls in the Marines with twenty-four months in various combat zones. No one knew it was a small town in the Berkshire Hills of Western Massachusetts that gave him nightmares. Being in a quaint country village and almost getting cut in half by a shotgun blast was not what he had expected. The "BOOM" he heard when he hit his head, he thought was from the impact on the pavement only to learn later it was a blast from a shotgun. Who knew that slipping on black ice getting out of the cruiser would save his life? Lying there on the ground dazed gave the shooter the impression that he had hit his target and the deed was done. The false sense of security and the relative peacefulness of the mountains hid secrets that no one was supposed to know about. The FBI had cautioned Danny not to talk about the situation back home while at the FBI National Academy. Yes, it was in the news; but they were controlling what got out. The FBI did not want more information than they deemed necessary to be made public until they were ready. If word got out about Danny being the target of a mob hit, then there would be a ton of questions. Danny was surrounded by several hundred high ranking police officers who were used to getting answers. Danny would be informally but relentlessly interrogated by his classmates. So, for the time being, he was to maintain a low profile and not standout. But people were talking. The sound of the reoccurring nightmares had extended beyond the room. The two suitemates who shared the bathroom heard all the noise and then the conversations with Mike. That opened the circle of people in the know and was a topic of conversation among the rest of the class. No one wanted a roommate who was having problems. They weren't afraid of Danny. They just wanted to study and get a decent night sleep without the animal sounds. There were some serious squirrels running around in that young man's head, and he needed to do something about it. The assignment to the FBI National Academy had gotten Danny out of town but not away from the dreams.

The Behavioral Science guys at Quantico were trying to help while they debriefed him, but there was only so much they could do. The counseling was there, but Danny refused any type of medication even if the FBI doctors said it was OK. Danny wanted his life back but on his own terms. He did not want the false safety blanket of drugs that he might become dependent upon to sleep the night through.

When Mike went to the FBI coordinators and asked for a new roommate, it was Danny who moved, not him. The agents had speculated about the dreams, but Mike finally confirmed it. Danny was given his own room and had sole use of the bathroom. It was just like all the rooms in the dormitories. There were two beds, two desks with chairs, two sitting chairs with bare walls. The rooms were plain but totally functional. A few of the females had put up posters and other decorations. The guys would not get past a picture or two on their desks. A few had their notes carefully taped to the walls with painter's tape so that the paint wouldn't peel off when they left. With no one else in the room, Danny had a classical radio station playing music all night long. Mozart, Beethoven, and other long dead composers' sounds played softly through the night. Even the disc jockey had a soothing voice. This helped; most of the dreams were gone, most of them. But erasing the past several years was not going to happen overnight, if ever. He had always kept the demons at a distance, but sleep let them creep in and take over his thoughts. The unexpected things that went on in Maidstone surprised him more than the events in a combat zone. Yes, they could both be deadly, but in the Middle East it was expected. It was a surprise in the Berkshire Hills. A small-town police officer wasn't supposed to be the target of a mob hit. But that is what happened, and Danny had no control over it.

Chapter 2

The two and a half months at the FBI National Academy in Quantico were ending for Danny Gilcrest. His time away from Maidstone, Massachusetts, had been well spent but now reality was setting in. After all that had happened, could he go back, did he want to go back? The college campus grounds and atmosphere of the academy gave a sense of security and isolation. He was protected. Tucked into some pine trees on a far corner of the Marine Corps Base, security was tight; students and faculty were ladies and gentlemen. There were no loud parties, and everyone concentrated on doing their best. Everything was organized, controlled, and structured. Danny was being taught by some of the best in law enforcement, and he was getting paid. He grabbed a couple of beers and headed down to the boat house just a short walk from the academy grounds. He had a lot of thinking to do and some decisions to make--decisions that needed to be sooner rather than later. It was spring in Virginia, and everything was coming back to life. The grey of winter was almost gone, and things were starting to bloom and turn green. Pretty soon it would get hot and humid but right now things were just perfect--not too warm and not at all cold.

Who would think that slipping on ice and nearly fracturing his skull would save his life? If he hadn't flipped out of the cruiser door that icy night, the shotgun blast would have caught him in the head and that would have been the end of it. But he had slipped, and the blast went over him and not into him. The hit man thought that what he saw was a full direct hit on his target with twelve pellets of double O buck shot finding their mark taking the police officer down forever.

But here in Quantico at the Marine base where the FBI academy is located, things had become somewhat isolated from everything that was happening in Massachusetts. Life was going on in both places but now separated by time and distance that made wanting to go back less and less attractive. It was nice of the FBI and the Massachusetts State Police to get Geri a spot in one of the classes down here at the Academy if only for a week. Back then he wasn't sure if she was ever going to see him again after almost getting her killed. Once it was confirmed that Danny had been taken out, the hit team would finish the job. Trooper Geri Anyzeski and District Attorney Marvin Cohen would be eliminated. The plan fell apart when the blast missed Danny. Geri got a warning phone call from an FBI wiretap just moments before two thugs kicked in her door. It was just enough time to grab her 38 snuby and take cover behind the kitchen counter. The first mutt through the door took one right in the snot locker and dropped like a rock. The second guy didn't even have time to get his gun up when Geri put two dead nuts in the K-5. Even after all that, Geri did show up at Quantico with his smiling yellow Labrador, Bear; and after all the crap back in Maidstone, she had missed him as much as he had missed her. Now she was back on the job with the state police, and contact was now just emails and phone calls.

Bob Marshall School of Forestry in Saranac Lake, New York, was sounding better every time he thought about it. The school looked more like an Adirondack resort than a college campus. Getting in there had been his goal all along, but

8

playing cops and robbers in Maidstone had gotten him side tracked and almost killed. If he went to Bob Marshall, what would he do about Geri? She had a good job as a trooper with the Massachusetts State Police and leaving just to be with him didn't seem fair. Getting out of the Marines and into Bob Marshall had been the perfect and simple plan; at that point, things got complicated. He needed college credits to get in and a job to support him. No big deal until the police department came along and offered him a better paying job. There was the college education he was getting, but not the one that Bob Marshall would give him. It would not be the final career of working in the woods. Then Geri came along, and things went more sideways than he had ever imagined. Who knew he would fall in love with a female state trooper with an attitude? And if things couldn't get more complicated, there was the murder, a horrible murder that took place in a quiet New England town. He couldn't have imagined that two people he went to high school with would end up with one being the victim and the other a murderer or that Danny would be part of it. Most of that was behind him now, but soon he would be back to the Berkshires. There would be pending court cases or, at the least, several hearings if people wanted to cut a deal or just plead guilty. He had heard rumors that some of the events were blamed on him--not for committing an offense but for not looking the other way and letting things pass and get back to normal. A murder had happened, but it was ruled a domestic that had gotten out of hand and a suicide. The shotgun had accidently discharged. Now Penelope (Copper Penny) Worthington was dead. A tragic time…but for everyone in town it was over. It was time to move on, but Danny hadn't let it go. If he had, he wouldn't have been shot at. He would never have been sent to the FBI National Academy. If he let it go, then he would still be in

9

Maidstone, Massachusetts, living the good life in the Berkshires and seeing Geri a lot more frequently. But that didn't happen, and now Danny had to make decisions and soon. He had been at the boat house for better than an hour and was right back to square one, trying to make some sense out of the events and ultimately come to a decision. Danny had come full circle to the beginning without moving one step closer to deciding his future.

Danny was thinking that he should just chuck the whole thing and get over to Saranac Lake and Bob Marshall and do what he set out to do. But that would mean leaving Geri and the Berkshires and running away from Maidstone. If he did that, then it would look like he had done something wrong. People would think that he had something to hide, that he was running away from the truth. That's not what Marines do; they take it head-on until they accomplish their missions. Six years in the Marines had taught him many things. He knew he had to go back until this was finished, to see where this would take him and Geri. He had to get to a real end, and this wasn't it. Bob Marshall would still be there. His thoughts and a plan were in the most roundabout way coming together, and he didn't even know it.

The beer was gone, and the sun was getting low. It was time to head back to the dorm and see about dinner. A direction had been chosen, and it was his decision. While it was his to make, life has a way of putting a spin on things. Other people were making decisions too that would have an effect on Danny's life, where it would go and what would happen. Every person who ever carried a rifle into battle knows that no good plan survives first contact. Danny had a plan, a simple plan, but other people had a vote as to what the outcome could be. Danny had a plan before and made slight changes, changes that almost got him killed. Well, that was behind him or at least that was what he thought. What else could go wrong in a sleepy little town tucked into the Berkshire Hills?

Chapter 3

Arriving back at his dorm room, he saw a note taped to the door telling him to call Special Agent Deverse. He wasn't one of the agents who had debriefed him or one of the instructors, so Danny was curious about who this guy was and why he needed to talk to him. Danny made the call; the conversation was brief. They were to meet up in the lounge and over a couple of beers and talk about heading home. The conversation was about what Danny was going to do once he had finished his training cycle at the academy.

"Sorry, you can't stay at Quantico forever," said Deverse.

Danny figured that once the courses wrapped up that he would pack his bags and be off. But the FBI had slightly different ideas for his future, ideas that would not be completely disclosed.

Tom Deverse was an easy-going guy and just a bit over weight for an FBI agent, but he was up there in the ranks and well thought of. He knew all about Danny, Geri and Maidstone but did not let on that he was in on all the details. They sat down and had a couple of Strohs and started with light conversation. Danny was not too keen on opening up and gave mainly *yes* and *no* answers to the polite conversation regarding the weather, the training and such. Tom Deverse realized that bonding with this guy wasn't going to happen in a few words, so he got straight to the point. Down the road they would be talking so forcing things into a close relationship now wasn't necessary. But Tom Deverse knew they would be talking, a lot.

"Danny boy, you are heading home to a slightly different Maidstone. Some things you are going to like and other things not so much. The FBI has been in town interviewing everyone. The town being just a tad on the rich and educated side has bent over backwards to pledge their full and complete cooperation, but…...."

"Yeah, but what?"

"They pledge full and complete cooperation once their attorneys have come to an agreement with the Justice Department. In other words, they have circled the wagons and no one is saying a thing but……"

"Ok, but what?"

"We have been hitting nerves and making people show some deep concern. Several people from the police department including the chief have decided on a career change. The chief has decided it is time to retire. We were never able to connect him to the cover up or the attempted murder. Then again, he had to know about Detective Lieutenant Snyder's outside activities and the use of law enforcement assets at the town's expense. The chief chose not to do anything. As far as the murder and the cover-up, he took no action to see that the case was handled properly. In short, he would be looking at dereliction of duty but more importantly unauthorized use of the computer system and state and federal funds. Those we have a good chance of proving. His actions or in-actions bought him his retirement."

"A few officers who might have been involved have moved on, but we haven't proved it yet. There are others that didn't want to be tainted by the corruption of the department for the rest of their careers, so they went to other PDs. We also had one dispatcher, a records clerk, and two people at the district attorney's office look for greener pastures. The investigation isn't over, and progress is slow with no one except you fully cooperating. We do have a couple of arrests pending, but I can't go into that."

Almost as an afterthought he said, "In addition, a number of people in the town are not happy with you."

Danny heard the statement, but could not comprehend how that could be. Geri had mentioned it, but he didn't take her seriously.

"You mean as part of the murder or the cover up?"

"Only in the remotest sense, you took out LT Snyder. Actually, he took himself out, but they blame you."

"Blame me for what? He tried to get me killed and covered up a murder."

"You took out the fixer and the money man."

Danny was staring at the agent trying to understand the statement.

"You don't get it, do you? Anyone who had a problem in town went to Snyder, not the chief. It didn't matter if it was a speeding ticket, a DUI arrest, or a problem with some guy a daughter was dating. Snyder took care of things. The out-of-town people came to rely on him for his security services. Through him country homes were rented on a regular basis for more money than the going rate. The property managers knew when the owners would not be around. If, let's say, they knew the owners were in Europe for the summer, the house might get rented out off the books with the property manager pocketing the whole fee. This trickled down to food service, the maintenance people, and off-duty police officers—all because Snyder brought in out-of-towners. The locals don't like the fact that Penny was murdered or that Snyder had covered it up and are very sympathetic to you almost getting killed. But in the end, you are costing them big bucks. They were making good money, and you killed the goose that laid the golden egg, so to speak. It isn't like you are in danger from them like you were with Snyder. But they see you as the person who turned off easy cash."

Danny was trying to digest what was being said and where he stood in the eyes of Maidstone. He felt betrayed. Were they that self-centered that they only cared about themselves and could write off the life of Penny Worthington, a person they knew? Everyone has their own agenda, their priorities, but this was a just a bit over the top.

"Don't get me wrong, there are a lot of people back there who support you, but there is this group of alleged solid citizens who aren't thrilled with the most recent events. They were happy to see a quick arrest when Brad, the murdering husband, was picked up the first time. They were even happier when it was all over without a lengthy trial and the town being held up to scrutiny. There was no court room testimony about the extra marital affairs or the full-blown sex parties. Now with the truth coming out, Maidstone isn't looking like the perfect artsy fartsy/hipster dipster town they think it is, an image they wanted people to believe. The guilty plea and probation put the incident behind them. It ended quietly with no high-profile trial or news crews creating sound bites every night. With the plea and quick end, national news wasn't out walking the streets trying for comments from the locals about what had happened in this small New England town. Everyone was ready to move on, but you turned the town on their heads and *bam*, they are back in the news."

Danny couldn't help but shake his head and wonder what had ever happened to the town he had grown up in.

"Now there is a bright side. There is a new chief; and he is from out of town, way out of town. He is a retired Army Lieutenant Colonel who was in the Military Police Corps. He has his BA in history from Holy Cross and received his JD from John Jay while in the army. He attended the National Academy a bunch of years back. He has been the chief of a small town in New Hampshire for three years. There are also several openings in the department with Snyder being gone and several other retirees. People have moved on so there is a chance for a promotion for you. The opportunity exists for the department to turn around and move on in a better direction. The new chief has orders from the town council to clean things up, and they are not going to get in the way with the Justice Department and the FBI still investigating and looking over their shoulders. Some of those on the town council, while not a target of the investigation, are feeling the heat. There are a lot of people who should have known and might have known what was going on--they looked the other way. For them, Snyder was a problem solver, and some people were very happy with the results if not the process."

Danny though about what had been said. Deverse, seeing the look on Danny's face, stayed quiet as he could see the wheels turning.

Chapter 4

Maidstone is a quiet town, a nice town with good people, thought Danny. They are the quiet ones, the ones who don't need special help. Those citizens don't have the *money buys you extra privileges* attitude and want a town that's just a beautiful little New England village with charm and peace. That was what most of the town was like. The small-town feeling was what brought Danny back after the Marines because he wanted that in his life. He wanted the small-town charm that didn't stink of garbage, diesel fumes, human waste, and dirt in the air all the time. He wanted blue skies and mountains, four seasons with rain, snow, changing leaves and budding plants. At least that was still there, but the people were another thing.

With a deep sigh, he turned to Tom Deverse and as part statement and part question said, "I am going back. I don't know for how long or what I intend to accomplish, but I am going to give it a shot. I still have Bob Marshall in the back of my mind but after that, then what? I don't think I am ready for a promotion, and I still have a lot to learn. If there is an exam, I will take it if for no other reason than the practice to see what it is all about. I have to be close to the most junior member of the department so realistically I don't see a promotion anytime soon."

"Danny boy, don't sell yourself short. We, as in the FBI, the Justice Department, and the district attorney know a lot about you; and it is all good. Kinda rough around the edges and needing polish, but it's all good."

"What do you mean that you know a lot about me?"

Agent Deverse crossed his arms and rested back in his chair. He was exploring his options, what to reveal and what to hold back. The FBI was never known for direct candor. They always hedged their bets and held back something or everything. Deverese was trying to figure out how far he could go. The information they knew about Danny was that he was a good kid, a good Marine, and a good, honest police officer. Unfortunately, there was always a *but*. All that was good was about yesterday and today--the *but* was about tomorrow. What about the dreams? This whole thing in Maidstone could have turned him. It could have been the proverbial last straw--when a good person goes bad and says *Screw it, I want my part.* Danny did not appear to be at that stage, but no one could predict if or when that day might come. The FBI didn't trust anyone, not even their own people. So Deverse decided to go with the public record and not all the details the Behavioral Science Unit at Quantico had come up with, which was a lot. Danny thought he was being debriefed, and in a way he was. But the Behavioral guys went far beyond debriefing regarding the case and were trying to see what made Danny tick. They wanted to know where his breaking point was. They weren't done exploring.

"Let's go over your track record." The tone now was more professional, less personal and more direct. "You did just enough to graduate from high school and then entered the Marines."

Danny though about that and had to admit that he didn't do very well in high school. It was boring and not much of a

18

challenge. He passed his courses not to learn anything but to keep playing sports. Toward the end of high school, the Marine Corps recruiter told him he had to have a high school diploma to get into the Marines. So, he stuck it out and graduated. Danny, with a slight shoulder shrug, nodded his head in agreement.

"Then you got to beautiful Parris Island where all of a sudden you start doing exceptionally well on the military IQ examines and maxing all of your training tests. Your physical fitness tests were all in the top end, and you ended up helping other people through boot camp."

Danny thought about those twelve weeks; and, yes, he had always scored well at least on paper. But the drill instructors were always on him to do better. Even when he scored 95 or 100, he came away with the feeling that he hadn't done enough and had to try harder. He said as much to Deverse.

"Do you know why they kept pushing you when you got a score of 100?"

Danny shook his head, "No clue. I have to guess that they were just being as big a pain in the ass as possible."

"Because they could see that you had more than a 100 score in you, and they wanted it all. You ended up mentoring other less gifted Marine recruits, didn't you?"

"Yes."

"Did the honor graduate of your platoon get to mentor other recruits?" Deverse wanted to know. He already knew the answer.

After thinking long and hard the answer was, "No."

"Do you know why you were not the honor graduate?"

Again, Danny's answer was, "No."

"Because they already had two white guys in two other platoons, and they had to spread the awards around in the other two platoons." Deverse waited for the answer to sink in.

Danny was dumbfounded. He never considered that the Marines would even think of something like that much less take part in it. The recruit who had been selected was a pretty good troop, but there were others who had higher scores. Danny rattled off three names of recruits in his platoon who were better than the one who had been selected.

"Pay attention. Two of those guys you are pointing out are white and the other is black and one of the other platoons already had a black honor graduate. Hello, are you listening?"

Danny couldn't believe the Marine Corps would do that, but now with the new information it all fit. It sucked big time, but it fit. Danny shook his head and all he could say was, "Unbelievable."

Deverse continued. "While not being the honor graduate, your records revealed just what a good recruit you had been. That continued on throughout your six years in the Marines. You always got promoted on time if not slightly sooner, and you were normally working in a position one pay grade above what your rank was, isn't that correct?"

Danny thought about that. When he was a Corporal, he was doing a Sergeant's job; and when he was a Sergeant, he had been doing a Staff Sergeant's job. He just had thought that the Marines were short on people and not inclined to give out promotions.

"Remember after your second combat tour when you put in for Marine Barracks Groton so you could be in New England and closer to home and maybe get some skiing in?"

How did he know about Groton and skiing, thought Danny? But he just shrugged his shoulders, "Yeah, so?"

"Well, when you put in the request the Company Commander went to the Battalion Commander, and they both agreed that they wanted you running a platoon teaching a Second Lieutenant how not to get himself and his people killed. They were not about to waste you in a guard detachment at a submarine base."

Danny could not believe what he was hearing. The back-door deals and the amount of information that the FBI had was a bit unnerving. Just how far had the FBI gone, and how much of his life was an open book--a life controlled by others without his knowledge. Danny was about to put a stop to this and demand answers, but it dawned on him that this was all history. He couldn't stop anything. The FBI had done his whole history in more detail than Danny knew about himself. In most cases he knew what had happened to him, but these guys knew the *why* which he was not always privy to.

"How in the world did you find all this out?"

"When a person, civilian or military, especially military, gets called into a room with two FBI agents, certain promises are made. Other threats are implied, and guarantees are made so people start talking just to get out of the room. Your drill instructors, platoon leaders, and company commander were all very willing to talk and all spoke very highly of you. When they found out it was you that we were looking into, they were more than happy to talk because none of it was controversial. They had only good things to say. The honor graduate selection was out of their hands, so they had no problem giving that up. When it came to the company and the battalion commanders' decision to turn down your request, it was for the good of the Corps. So, they thought they were totally justified."

Danny could not decide if this were all good or all bad or possibly something else. He never knew his life would be so questioned or examined in this kind of detail. Danny though of Ray, a great guy from 2nd Air-Naval-Gunfire Liaison Company. Danny had escorted Ray in the field a few times. Ray would be on the radio calling in naval gunfire or close air support. His voice was so calm that it reminded Danny of a guy calling for a pizza when in reality he was calling for a couple of 500-pound bombs to drop 1,000 meters from where they were standing. Ray wasn't a hard-charging Marine, but he was a good Marine. If the shit were flying, Ray would always come up with the line, "I am just a poor, poor lad, trying to make his way through a troubled, troubled world."

All Danny could think was *Ray, I am with ya, brother*, especially now sitting with Agent Deverse and hearing his life history from someone else's perspective.

Deverse broke Danny's day dream and continued. "Besides the promotions and assignments ahead of other Marines, you also racked up some awards. The write ups for those are very impressive."

"It is what we all did," cut in Danny, "and I didn't do any of those things alone. I had a lot of help."

"Yes, you did have a lot of help. You led and your team, squad and later your platoon all followed you. I emphasize *followed* because all the write ups have you leading from the front--not giving orders and watching your Marines move out."

"Leading from the front is what Marines do."

"That's what Marines are supposed to do," countered Deverse. "Not all of them do that. Some of them do, but not all the time. You did it all the time. From the write ups, the fact that you are still up and talking with only a limited number of holes in your body is just short of a miracle."

"Like I said, I had a lot of help; and the guys looked out for me."

"Yes, they did and for good reason. Now let's talk about college. For a guy who just made it out of high school, you are doing well in college, high honor grades. Not bad for a guy who didn't like school. How did that happen?" Deverse already knew but he wanted to hear it from Danny.

"Some of the foundation I needed for the college courses I picked up in the Marines, specifically math. The fact that I had to do well if I ever wanted to get into forestry school was also a motivator. Even if I didn't like the course, I had to do well first to get in and then second to be able to do that job. Taking law enforcement courses built on the reserve officers' law enforcement classes I had already taken to become a certified police officer. So, I had exposure to the information before I took the course. The regular students were starting from scratch. I had a leg up on them."

"Are you seeing a trend here?"

"Yes, I do. I see the FBI checking out every aspect of my life in extreme detail and to what end?"

That wasn't the answer Deverse was looking for but had to admit, "You are correct, but there is another point--the point where you are working and succeeding way above what you think you can do. A leader who doesn't know he is a leader. Have you thought about that?"

"No," was the quick answer.

"Well, you have and that continued on into your work in law enforcement. I would have said your career in law enforcement, but you keep telling people that you are going to forestry school. Your being a police officer is only a bridge to get into Bob Marshall. While you have been saying that from the beginning, somehow three years have passed. You had the credits you needed a while back, but you stayed in Maidstone. You kept taking courses instead of heading off to the Saranac Lake region. Why is that?"

23

They did know a lot about him, thought Danny. He had never looked back that far or that hard. He never made a detailed plan. He had one, but it kept changing. He didn't analyze his decisions; he just made them and moved on.

"I guess there were a number of reasons that I didn't spend much time thinking about it. First was the fact that while I wasn't over in New York State going to school, I was building college credits. Of course, there was the money. The VA benefits, the Marine Corps League Scholarship and the Veterans Scholarship provided more money than college cost. My education was free, and I was making more money going to school than I would in New York. Police work paid better than a minimum wage job they would have found for me at Bob Marshall. I live in a relatively free apartment on the estate, and the owners were almost never there. Granted it was an apartment in a barn but very un-barn like. The apartment has 600 square feet of living space with hand-me-down furniture from the main house. While used furniture, I couldn't even think of affording the pieces like those. All I had to do was keep an eye on the place and minor maintenance when the caretakers or contractors couldn't get there. Not many guys my age have that kind of a deal. If I went to New York State, I would be living in a dorm room with at least one other guy. I got comfortable with my own place even if I didn't own it. Being a police officer was nothing like I imagined it would be. I never thought I would be trying to solve so many people's problems or that someone could even think I had the answers. Police work is fun, challenging, different, a lot of things that you don't get in a normal job."

Chapter 5

Deverse was taking it all in, but Danny Boy was leaving a big detail out--really two big details. Deverse wanted to hear it but wanted Danny to bring it up. He sat there quietly looking at Danny not saying a word. Silence is way to get the other person talking.

After numerous seconds of dead air, the subject being questioned begins to feel a need to say something, to counteract the empty space, to fill the void especially when there is more to be said. Deverse kept looking at him. He made no effort to prompt him into speaking. The silent look would be enough to move things along.

Deverse just had to be patient and wait. It took a lot for him not to jump in and get things going. But he didn't, and finally the silence got to Danny. It dawned on him what Deverse was waiting for. He wasn't sure if he wanted to share those feelings with the FBI. But they already knew, so what was the point? They knew enough about Danny to get his girlfriend State Trooper Geri Anyzeski and his Labrador Bear down to Quantico for a training class while he was there. They also arranged for them to meet at the Major's Place where Danny had made a promise to the Major the last time he was there. He told the Major that he would be returning with a lovely young lady for dinner the next time. That first time had been years ago, but somehow, they knew. Danny looked at

Deverse who returned the gaze. He gave a shoulder shrug and a what-gives hand gesture knowing that Danny had just figured out where this was going.

"Yeah, you're right."

"Right about what?" He wasn't giving an inch. He wanted to hear it and know they were right about Danny.

With a deep sigh Danny said, "Geri and Bear, I couldn't leave them. Things are going just too well. If I went to Bob Marshall, I would hardly see Geri and would have to leave Bear. The school wouldn't let me have Bear on campus, and I could not afford off-campus housing."

"In the list of things you just gave me, you listed them last. Why was that?"

"Because that is none of your business, but I now know that you know all of my business so what was the point of all this?"

"With that said, where would you put Geri and Bear?"

"You're an asshole, Tom."

"This might surprise you, but you are not the first person to point that out."

They both gave a small knowing laugh. Danny wasn't happy with the microscopic examination, but there wasn't anything he could do about it.

"Back to police work. Have you ever wondered why a junior patrolman keeps making leadership decisions when there are sergeants and lieutenants on duty?"

Truth be told, Danny hadn't thought about it until that very moment. Now he did. Agent Deverse let him think about that and did not interrupt his train of thought. Danny had a far-off look and was thinking back to some of those decisions. Three years of decisions were going through his mind reliving some crazy days and nights on the job. Agent Deverse just let him take his walk down memory lane and watched the expression on Danny's face change and his hands move as he recalled deep in thought those decisions. At times his jaw would clench, and other times the brow would crease, and the lips became tight. Danny was thinking and thinking hard. That was a good thing, thought Deverse, but he didn't want to lose him to the past. Deverse was thinking about interrupting as time was going by. Danny had more than enough time to review a number of incidents to help him determine why he did what he did. And then Danny was back. The far-off look disappeared, and he locked eyes with Deverse.

"No one else was making any decisions, so I did."

"Were you always right?"

"No," was the quick answer.

"Excellent," was Deverse's response.

"You like the fact that I made mistakes?" Danny asked with a puzzled look on his face.

"Screwing up--that's not good. Knowing that you screwed up and admitting it is good. Too many people like to hide from their mistakes and cover things up. Admitting that some of your decisions were mistakes shows that you evaluate what you do and don't give yourself a pass when you get it wrong."

"Are you with the behavioral guys or are you an agent?"

"If you stay in the bureau long enough, the behavioral stuff rubs off on you. Being an investigative unit for the justice department and the US attorney, we are always analyzing what is being said and why. It's our job to talk to people and find out the standard who, what, when, where, why, and how. We have to know when someone is telling the truth and when they are not. In your case, what you see is what you get. That isn't always the case with other people especially cops and their business associates, the robbers. It is hard to get a straight-forward answer from either group.

"Your college studies are going extremely well, but you still have a way to go for your bachelor's degree. There are some people who hope that happens sooner rather than later and that you might be interested in applying for a position with the bureau. No guarantees mind you, but you are already known to a number of people who could be a positive influence on getting an appointment. Your background has been done and there are no problems there. Do you think you might want to join the bureau?"

Danny was about to blurt out, hell yes, thinking of all the great training, resources, and assignments. The down side was that the training was here in Quantico, and his first posting with the FBI would be at one of the major field offices. He would have a good chance of getting New York City if not at first but down the road. But Danny had no desire to work in New York City or Chicago, Kansas City, Detroit, LA, DC or Miami.

"I don't know," admitted Danny. "I have lived all over the country and the world, and I love the Berkshires. Extending from the Berkshires, I love New England and upper New York State. You can keep the Big Apple. After the Marines all I wanted to do was get back into the woods and have four real seasons with all the good and bad weather. I don't know if I could hold out long enough in a major field office trying to get back to New England. There just are not enough positions up there with a lot of guys applying for them. The training would be great and the assignments interesting; but to live in or near Detroit for three to six years, I just don't know."

"At least think about it and keep the idea in mind. Maidstone is a small town, and it isn't going to get much bigger. Are you tight with the guys in the PD?"

Danny cocked his head to one side and thought for a moment. "Not really, I guess. I get along with just about everyone, but most of the guys and ladies on the job don't have my life style. Very few ski and none of them cross country ski or snowshoe. None of them think camping out is fun unless you have an RV with a complete water and electric hookup plus satellite TV. Most don't think that college is all that important, and a number have second jobs to make ends meet. They work two jobs to get their kids through college. They are all nice people for the most part; we just have different interests."

"Well, I hope you had a good time here at the NA. See you around."

There was the handshake, and both knew that they would be seeing each other sometime soon.

Chapter 6

Graduation was a quiet affair. There weren't many family members mostly just the NA grads and the staff from the Academy. A few who lived close by in the greater DC area had family attend. Most people were scattered all over the country and to travel all that way for a one-hour graduation didn't seem realistic. As soon as the graduation was over, every student would be headed for home by the quickest route. Some would be loading up cars and others catching the shuttle to the airport. No one was hanging around. A small section of the Marine Corps Band was there to add pomp to the ceremony. The Director of the FBI and an official from the Justice Department would be there to present the diplomas.

As Danny made his way through the line to receive his diploma, he could hear the standard lines coming from the director and the DOJ official: congratulations, nice job, and good luck in the future. Followed by a quick handshake and the slight turn to the camera, the graduate and the director could be captured smiling, shaking hands, and looking straight into the camera with the diploma exchanging hands. With a slight step to the right, this was repeated with the DOJ rep. Then it was off the stage and repeated with the next graduate. These pictures would soon be hanging in every graduate's office back at their respective police departments. These guys were all ranking officers most with fifteen or more years of police service. Danny would have a picture, but hanging it in his cruiser just wouldn't work. Danny did not see an office in his future.

Greeting after greeting was repeated, and then Danny made his way on stage when his name was called. He saw the director of the FBI hesitate for a second as the assistant called out his name and handed the director the diploma. The director extended his hand just as he had done with every graduate; but instead of the standard line and the quick hand shake, the grasp was extended beyond the normal formality of shaking hands.

"Outstanding job, Officer Gilcrest, outstanding," was his comment.

Danny wasn't sure what to say but used the old standard, "Thank you, Sir." He had done well at the academy, but he was no super star just a good solid *A* student. Most of the graduates fit into the same category. The classes were well taught. The instructors were always available for extra help, and studying was the norm, not partying all night. The graduates were all professionals; and while there are always a few screw ups in any class, there were far fewer here than in a normal college setting.

While still shaking his hand, the director turned to the DOJ representative and introduced Officer Danny Gilcrest to him. Now the cameraman was trying to get "THE" picture with Danny and the director, but they kept moving and not facing the camera. When the rep from Justice heard the name, he also held out his hand replacing the director's and in turn thanked Danny for a job well done. The director now had his arm over Danny's shoulder and kept saying nice things, but Danny couldn't hear much as he was trying to figure out what was going on. He was ready for the standard hand shake, the slight turn, and the photo and then be off the stage. That wasn't happening. He had his diploma and tried to keep moving but the two officials had him blocked in. Finally, the photographer gave a cough, and the two officials came back into character with the standard photo. Once again, they changed things up. This time they had Danny stand between them for some additional photographs. Finally, Danny was free to go with a pat on the back from the director and the justice department rep. Once Danny was off the stage, everything went back to the normal routine for the rest of the graduates. The officers filed back to their seats and waited for the last diploma to be awarded.

On Danny's left was the chief of a medium sized police department in Ohio.

"Ok, Gilcrest, what the hell was that all about?"

With that a captain from Chicago PD on his right joined in. "You related to someone we don't know about?"

All Danny could say was, "Beats the shit outa me."

"Right," said the chief, not believing it.

"You're sandbagging us," said the captain.

Other graduates were also wondering what was up with Gilcrest. Being one of the most junior officers in the class and the only one without even a sergeant rank made him stand out a little at first but no one really questioned it. But now with the special attention from the Director of the FBI and one of the Assistant US Attorneys in the Justice Department, interest had piqued, and eyebrows were raised. Who was this guy Gilcrest, the class wanted to know? Danny had never mentioned the incident back in Maidstone.

Fortunately for Danny when the graduation ceremony was over, everyone had getting home on their mind. There were still a few people who took the time to come up and pump Danny for information—information he didn't have or at least wouldn't reveal. Back in his dorm room his former

32

roommate was full of questions. He was also doing some last-minute packing and concentrating on getting to the airport on time. The shuttle was leaving with or without him and getting home was priority number one.

"Well," he asked Danny, "the director and an assistant US attorney want a picture with you and not the other 300 or so graduates. What is up with that?"

"I am just as surprised as you and everyone else. I worked one small assignment with the FBI, so it isn't like I have a lot of friends in the bureau. I have never even seen those two before today when I walked on the stage."

Danny's former roommate was one more disbelieving individual. That was very special attention for a regular police officer. The class was full of chiefs of police, deputy chiefs, and all kinds of senior ranking officers from across the country and junior here gets star treatment. Maybe someday I will find out, maybe someday, he thought. "Well, I guess I am on my way before I miss the bus. You have my email so stay in touch, Danny Boy. At some point you are going to have to explain all that to me."

Danny shook hands, and his roommate beat a hasty exit. Danny thought about the graduation and the additional attention. Maybe I do have a shot at getting down here again, but do I want to? Well, that decision is way down the road. Getting a degree going part-time is going to take a while. Even if I wanted to be an agent that has to be accomplished first before I can even apply.

Danny loaded the last items into his Jeep and said good bye to Tom Deverse. He drove around the academy grounds one more time taking it all in. The money that was spent to train police officers and special agents had to be huge. This was like no other police academy Danny had ever seen. One thing that stood out was that nothing was ever trashed. Unlike a college campus, everyone here was older and professional, so things were never damaged. Trash always made it into a proper container. No one walked on the grass, so this place would never get worn down only improved on. It was also a safe place. There were no radio calls, no fights, no drugs and only a few attitudes. With all the brass down here, no one got out of line for very long. When they did, the pack of chiefs, commissioners, colonels, and such would step on the wayward soul; and soon things would be back to normal. It was something like a monastery, thought Danny, everyone devoted to the cause working together in one direction. He was going to miss that unity and the dedicated learning, but this wasn't the real world. He hoped this was going to help him with the real world.

Chapter 7

Danny exited the Marine Corps Base at Quantico and the FBI Academy and got on I-95 north for the ride home. It would be a long ride, and he would have time to think. The dogwood trees should be blooming along Route 8 in Connecticut all the way up to Maidstone. It should be a pretty ride. Danny called Geri on his cell phone. She knew it was graduation day, but he wanted to make sure she knew he was on his way and wanted to see her.

"Well hello, stranger, looking for a good time?" asked Geri.

"Why yes, I am looking for a good time. Is there anyone you can hook me up with?"

"Smart ass."

"Why thank you for noticing, but just in case you can't find anyone on short notice, are you still off tomorrow?"

"What do you have in mind?" The tone in Geri's voice was very questioning.

"I thought that we could meet, and I could make lunch for you."

"Meet, like at the barn?"

"No, I was thinking about York Lake at Sandisfield State Forest where we went kayaking. Around 2 o'clock would be good, if you can make it." Danny was praying for a *yes* hoping that things were still on with Geri, but one never knows.

Geri definitely wanted to see him, but didn't want to sound too eager, keep him guessing just a bit. "That sounds good to me, but why not your apartment or a nice restaurant?"

"I have been in a very nice but sterile academic environment for more than two months. I want to get outside and just look at the water--hopefully see the sun and maybe watch some geese go by. I have been inside way too long and need a nature fix." His voice sounded tired and drained.

"Is that all you need, a nature fix?" was the not so pleasant response from a slightly irate Geri. But most of the comment was just Geri being a pain in the ass.

"No, not just a nature fix. Could you bring Bear with you?" Two could play at this game, thought Danny, but he quickly added, "I really want to see Bear's chauffer. I heard she is really cute for a State Trooper."

"She is really cute and into martial arts, so you better watch it, bucko."

"Oh, you can be sure I will be watching it. So, what's new?"

"Well, there is the proverbial good news/bad news. You have a new chief."

"I know about the retired army colonel; they told me about it down in Quantico."

"That's the good news. But the bad news is that he isn't there yet. He has to complete a transfer of his current department up in New Hampshire. It seems that he made a promise to them to stay until they found a replacement, and he feels duty bound to keep his promise."

"Sounds like a good guy. So, what is the bad news?"

"You have a temporary chief at the department until the new guy gets there."

"And who would that be?"

"Lieutenant Lincoln Cornell is the acting Chief, and the town fathers love him," Geri said in a dripping, sarcastic voice.

Danny's heart sank. This was the same Lieutenant that no matter what happened he would never leave the station. When Danny called for help, Cornell never bothered to get in a cruiser to respond. Danny flashed back to an incident he could never forget and almost didn't survive. It was the time Danny went on what should have been just a routine noise complaint that turned into a knockdown, drag out, no-holds barred, guns-drawn fight for his life. The lieutenant never left the building even after the switch board lit up every line, and the dispatcher was getting a blow-by-blow description of the fight from several callers. The state police had called on the inter-agency hotline stating that they were responding and needed directions to the location. The lieutenant never made a move for the door.

On that day Danny had exited his cruiser and thought all he would have to do was get everyone to quiet down. After all, it was just a noise complaint. What he didn't know was that it was just a bit more than a noise situation and that the other two units in town were in the south end with a serious domestic disturbance.

Danny didn't know that the loud music had turned into beer can throwing. That led to two brothers jumping in a jeep and doing donuts in a neighbor's garden. In the process of trashing the garden, they had rolled the jeep. Being totally out of it, they rolled the jeep back over by hand. Danny asked everyone to separate, but one individual just wasn't going to cooperate in any way. He tried to move him back with a gentle shove and a warning about being arrested. The response was six or more punches to Danny's head before he realized that he was being hit. Danny took a couple of steps back. He drew his side handled baton and again warned the individual to back off. The suspect charged, and Danny beat the crap out of him with almost no visible effect. The suspect took a few steps back, and Danny thought that he had gained the upper hand and was now taking control. He had hit the guy more than a half dozen times in the arms and torso area. He should have been one hurtin' individual. Instead the suspect ran backwards into a shed and came out with a 4x4 piece of lumber that was close to six feet long. In disbelief, Danny watched as the guy made his way out of the shed making a beeline for him. He came at Danny waving it like it was a small stick and was aiming for Danny's head.

Danny dropped the baton and in one quick motion got the cap-stun out and sprayed the suspect square in the eyes at a distance of a few feet. Cap-stun normally drops a person in their tracks. The spray causes them to lose vision and start gagging, coughing, and feeling like they are on fire. It did have some effect but only like squirting water in a person's eyes. There was no instant incapacitation. There was almost no reaction to the burning chemical.

Danny dropped the cap-stun, took a few steps back, pulled the Taser and fired directly into the guy's chest. The darts went right through the crazy man's thin tee shirt and imbedded themselves in his scrawny chest. The electric charge fired, and Danny waited for the guy to hit the ground. Instead of a collapsing suspect, Danny heard an animal roar. He watched in disbelief as the suspect ripped the darts out of his chest. He could see the electrical charge was still firing in the guy's hand with no effect.

Danny watched as the guy continued to roar. He made a fast pivot and ran into the house. The guy ran like a deer bounding across the grass covering several yards with each step. The beating, cap-stun, and Taser hadn't slowed this guy down one bit. If anything, this guy was more amped up now. Danny started to follow, but realized that this one guy was more than he could handle. If a night stick, Cap-stun and a Taser were not going to drop this guy down, then going in and wrestling with him was out of the question. Danny was strong; but after the beating he had laid on this guy with no affect, getting within grabbing distance would be fatal.

"HQ, I need help down here right away," Danny barked into the radio. "The situation is getting way out of hand and is more than one officer can handle."

As Danny finished the broadcast, someone from the crowd of neighbors shouted, "He is coming out with a gun!"

All Danny could think was that this can't be happening. He hoped he could hold on until the cavalry arrived. But that wasn't to be. The suspect exploded out the back door with what looked like a small caliber rifle, maybe a twenty-two. He was roaring all kinds of threats promising to kill everyone, and the cop was going to be first. He was waving the rifle around but so far had not lowered it in anyone's direction. Danny moved behind a tree and dropped to one knee drawing his Glock-17 and swinging it up on the target. The distance was less than 40 feet, and the suspect was standing in one position. It would have been impossible for Danny to miss.

"Drop the rifle and put your hands up. Put the rifle down and get on the ground now. Drop it now, or I will shoot!" Danny's commands brought no response as the suspect kept waving the rifle around and shouting at everyone.

Danny was in a protected location with a clear, steady aiming posture; and still the suspect screamed at Danny and the crowd. Then he began to lower the rifle in Danny's direction. As the rifle swung down, everything went into slow motion. Danny moved his finger inside the trigger guard and slightly closed his left eye sighting with his right. As the rifle moved lower, Danny stopped breathing and applied pressure to the safety inside the trigger. The safety was pressed, and the pressure was building on the trigger. At the last second the suspect pulled the bolt of the rifle to the rear revealing an empty weapon. Danny was only a few ounces of pressure away from putting a round in this guy's chest when he realized that the threatening and bluffing was with an empty friggin rifle. The weapon was thrown on the ground. The suspect stood there like a martyr waiting for the bullets to impact his chest. Staring into the sky, he continued to roar like an animal.

Danny holstered and moved out grabbing the guys left wrist, twisting it up and behind him, taking the suspect to the ground. The guy resisted, but the intensity was gone. The insane behavior of the past few minutes was beginning to subside. Danny was able to get the cuffs on him when he felt someone on his back reach for his holstered weapon. In less than a second, in his mind Danny could see the weapon coming out and rounds exploding from his own weapon tearing into his back. With all the desperation and strength he could muster, Danny wheeled around, slamming his elbow and upper arm into the person climbing on his back and sent him flying twenty feet to the side, rolling like a big snowball. Before the guy even stopped, Danny was on top, flipping the guy onto his stomach and pulling his arms behind him. The second set of handcuffs came out, and the guy was restrained.

"I was only trying to help," the guy pleaded. "I didn't do anything wrong."

After what had happened in those very few moments of an insane afternoon, Danny was not going to debate anyone. He had felt the guy on his back and his right hand reaching for his holstered weapon.

"Shut up. You are under arrest."

"But officer, please," he begged.

"Shut up or I will shut you up." Having managed to survive and not kill the psycho guy, Danny was in no mood to be nice to anyone. Danny was shaking, and now the cap-stun was starting to take effect—not on the suspect, but on Danny. He had rolled around cuffing the guy and now had cap-stun all over him.

Where the hell is my backup, Danny thought? He could barely see, and snot was running out of his nose and all over his shirt. His face was burning like it was on fire. He was coughing and gagging and spitting up all kinds of crap. Well, the shit works; but how the hell do I get out of here? I can't even see.

Finally, some of the spectators decided to get involved. Several people were holding the two brothers, and a few came over to see what they could do for Danny.

"Are you OK?" one of them asked.

"Do I look OK, or do I look like a puking firetruck? Is there a garden hose close by? I have to wash some of this stuff off, or I can't drive."

People were now all over the place bringing towels and water helping Danny and the two handcuffed brothers.

Where were all these people when I needed a hand when I was getting my ass kicked, Danny wondered? Where the hell is my back up?

After a few minutes no one had arrived, but Danny was starting to see a little bit and the gagging had stopped.

Danny pulled his portable radio from its holster and called the station.

"This is North Unit, where is my backup? I have two in custody, and I need transport and EMTs when we get to the station."

41

"Negative on the backup. The state police have been cancelled. Transport on your own," was the curt response.

Danny stared at the radio not believing what he had just heard. A few short minutes ago he was in a fight for his life and nearly killed a guy all the while thinking help was on the way. Danny was trying to make sense out of those last few minutes, soaking his face with the garden hose. He went over to the major player and began hosing him down. Somewhere after the rifle was pulled and they rolled around on the ground, whatever had over ridden the cap-stun and the Taser had finally warn off. He was in a million degrees of hurt, and the blows from the nightstick were now causing some serious pain. Of all the crazy things, the guy was now asking Danny for help. The lunatic was thanking him up and down for washing the cap-stun off of him. The brother was apologizing and insisted that he was only trying to help and not trying to take his gun.

Danny was taking it all in. The brother he had sent flying through the air seemed to be genuinely sincere in his statement that he was only trying to help. But as crazy as it sounded, so did the guy with the rifle. Just minutes before Danny was taking more blows than he could ever remember, fighting for his life against a raving lunatic bent on killing him. Now he was being thanked and getting apologies. More bystanders were gathering, and it appeared that another fight could start. People were voicing their opinions as to what was wrong and what was done and what should have been done. Tempers were starting to rise. Danny was starting to see, but really wasn't in a position to control a group of twenty or more. Then to his surprise, the guy he almost shot stepped in and took control. The suspect managed to get to his feet with the handcuffs on behind him and shouted at the crowd, "Would everyone just shut the hell up and go home. The officer was just doing his job, and we screwed up. So, if everyone would just go home, please."

Danny was hearing it, but not believing it. Even more astonishing was that the people quieted down and began to drift away. Danny stood and though half blind by the cap-stun, watched a near riot situation turn on a dime into a diminishing crowd. Then the suspect announced that they had better be off to the station before the people changed their minds.

Danny couldn't agree more, and the three staggered over to the cruiser and got in.

"Are you OK to drive?" asked the suspect.

One more astonishing moment, and of course the answer was, "Absolutely not, but we don't have another choice. Don't worry. I will drive slowly, and most people don't want to hit a cruiser."

Danny drove with his head out the window seeing just enough to keep in his own lane at twenty miles an hour. At the station the EMTs were standing by and were surprised at the condition of the three coming out of the vehicle. Danny, with the most clothes on, looked the worst. His face was bright red, and his eyes were almost swollen shut. There was blood, dirt, mud, grass stains, and sweat marks covering him from head to toe. While washing the cap-stun off of himself and the two arrestees, he had become soaked with water. Danny had been kneeling on the ground which had turned to mud. The EMTs assumed that Danny was bleeding from somewhere and were about to start cutting his shirt off when Danny told them that none of the blood was his and to see to the two arrestees. Everyone made their way inside and down to the cell block where the EMTs began to decontaminate the two prisoners and clean them up. Danny wanted to get into the bathroom and run more water, but there was no one to take charge of the prisoners. Finally, Lieutenant Cornell showed up in the cell block. His uniform and appearance were in direct contrast to the mess that Danny presented. Not a hair was out of place, and the white shirt seemed to glow it was so clean. The shoes shined bright, and the duty belt looked brand new without a mark on it.

Danny thought that Cornell was going to watch the prisoners and headed for the men's room only to be stopped by the lieutenant.

Chapter 8

"I have another call for you," the lieutenant announced.

Once more Danny could not believe what he was hearing but then thought that it must be something bad or important that the lieutenant would send him out after such a close call with death, his and a prisoner.

"What have you got?"

"There are a bunch of kids hanging around the town hall and the church next door, and we need to get them cleared out."

Looking through slits of eyes that saw everything in a pink glow, Danny stared at the lieutenant, thinking it was a joke and that the lieutenant was trying to lighten things up. He wasn't. He was dead serious. He wanted Danny heading out now, not after he cleaned up.

"The caller has been waiting for over thirty minutes and is getting impatient," continued the lieutenant. "We need the town hall cleared and for it to stay cleared once and for all. Make some arrests if you have to."

Danny starred with his mouth open trying to find words and bring some kind of understanding to what was being said considering what had taken place in the past hour. He could see down the front of his uniform just how bad he looked. He had even glanced at himself in the rear-view mirror of the cruiser, and he though he didn't look like himself or even human for that matter. Now I have to go arrest some kids for loitering on town property?

The lieutenant stood there expectantly, wondering when this guy was going to get moving. He made no comment about his appearance or the fact that Danny had just been in a fight for his life.

Danny wanted to find the words to tell him where to go, but he was just too beaten figuratively and literally. He decided that getting out of the station was his best option-- getting away from the lieutenant before he said or did something he would end up regretting. At least on the road he wouldn't have to see him or hear him. He wasn't about to arrest any kids for hanging out on the town green. Danny got a bottle of water from one of the EMTs and headed for the door. They tried to stop him, saying he really needed to get the cap-stun flushed out. Danny just raised the water bottle over his head and kept moving toward the door.

Danny took his time getting to the town green hoping that everyone would leave before he got there. Maybe when they saw the cruiser approach, they would take off. These weren't bad kids, just teenage pains-in-the-butt. They liked to hang around the town green smoking cigarettes and sneaking some wine in water bottles and plot the night's strategy, which wasn't much. Their main transgression was that some of the town elders didn't like seeing people on the town green or the litter and wear marks on the lawn they left behind. They were major criminals in some people's minds. These were just bored kids.

As he pulled up, they were still there, and the half dozen or so major offenders made no effort to move off the green. Danny pulled up the driveway about seventy-five feet from where the kids were sitting in a circle. They all saw the cruiser, but chose to pretend that it wasn't there. Danny hoped this would go easy and maybe, just maybe, a few words would clear them out. He rolled down the window and announced, "Ok, guys, everyone has got to go. You know you can't hang around here, so make some plans and take it somewhere else." The simple request didn't work. Teenage rebellion and stubbornness were in full defiant mode.

"What, officer? What did you say?" was the wise guy remark.

A tired and frustrated Danny gave it another shot.

"Guys, please, we have a complaint. I was sent down here, and you have to leave the green. Please, it has been a rough day; I don't want any hassles."

Being nice and asking nice wasn't working. Danny put the cruiser in park; and with an aching body, pulled himself from the vehicle. The defiant teens stood and prepared to stand their ground and face up to the Gestapo Trooper who was banishing them from their land. They knew their rights and were going to defend those rights. That was until they got a good look at Danny. As he slowly made his way towards the group, he asked them once more pleading with them to just leave. All stood there with mouths open. The mess that was Danny Gilcrest moved like a zombie towards them and appeared like something out of a bad horror movie. Danny, frustrated that they didn't just leave and let him catch just one little break, was about to unload. Danny was thinking that the first one who opened his mouth was going to take a pinch. The first one spoke, but it wasn't what Danny expected.

"Holy shit, officer, are you OK? Do you need an ambulance? Does anyone have a cell phone? Call an ambulance!"

"No, no, I am ok, no ambulance; but you guys have got to go," was Danny's response.

The group of defiant teens circled around Danny and walked him over to the steps of the town hall and set him down.

"You don't look OK, are you hurt? Someone get the cooler and water and ice. If anyone has a towel, get that, too." The kids who were about to defy the police were now scrambling in several directions. Danny was too tired and used up to make a protest. He was questioning his being sent there in the first place. A young lady was flushing his eyes out with water and another was holding ice on his face where he had taken so many punches just a short time ago. Hands were checking his body trying to figure out where all the blood had come from. Danny made no protest other than to say it wasn't his blood. After several minutes he was able to see more clearly, and the ice on his bruised face felt good. The kids still couldn't believe the mess they were looking at was a Maidstone police officer.

In a very tired voice, Danny said, "Guys, thanks for everything. I appreciate it, and I would like to sit here with you for the rest of the night. I have to go get cleaned up and get back to work. And please, I am begging you, please, find someplace else to hang out tonight, preferably where no one will see you."

"Yes, sir," came the quick reply. "Are you sure you are OK to drive?"

"I will be fine, I will just take it real slow."

"OK, we are outta here," and the teens loaded up their cars, but not before picking up the trash and giving Danny a bottle of water. Danny made his way back into the cruiser and called in that the town green was now clear, no arrests. He anticipated the usual "Roger" from the dispatcher, but instead he heard the lieutenant's voice wanting to know why it took thirty minutes to clear a few kids from the town green?

All kinds of responses came to Danny's mind, but he was smart enough not to hit the transmit key. Each response he thought of would have gotten him deeper in trouble and maybe even fired. He went with the old Marine Corps standard, "No excuse, sir."

"Get back in here. You have two prisoners to process."

This night is just never going to end. I really need to go and get cleaned up, he thought, but that wasn't going to happen. Everyone saw just how bad a night he had been through. The guys he arrested were worried about him. Then the pain-in-the-ass brats on the town green showed deep concern and compassion. Now the lieutenant wanted him to process the two prisoners. The lieutenant hadn't lifted a hand to help or call someone in to do the processing. Danny looked in the mirror and saw that now his face was really swollen, and the bruises were starting to turn color. He felt light headed and his vision was still not back. No, this shit stops right now; I have had enough. No more tough guy Marine sucking it up and driving on. The LT didn't care or appreciate what had happened or care about his condition. Cornell would keep his shirt nice and clean and his hair in that 1950s do with the gel.

Danny keyed the mike. "Dispatch, have the EMTs respond back to the station, I am not feeling well, and my vision is a mess."

There was a long pause before the dispatcher responded. All he said was a quiet, subdued, "Roger." In the background you could hear the lieutenant talking about what pussies the Marines were.

"Pussy is it?" Danny said to himself. "We shall see."

Danny got to the station before the EMTs did and with great effort, part real and part exaggerated, made his way into the station. He was unsteady on his feet but added to it just a

49

bit for affect. As he came near the dispatch center, he was walking supported by one hand on the wall. He did need assistance but not that much. As he imagined, that was when Cornell came out and was about to tear into him. The LT never saw it coming. Standing just inches away, he was about to say something when Danny, on his unsteady feet, stumbled forward right into the LT pushing him up against the wall. To anyone watching it would have looked like he just lost his balance for a second and the good LT was keeping him from falling. Danny regained his feet and apologized all over the place. The lieutenant looked at Danny and then at himself. In a split second the bright, clean white shirt was now covered in blood, dirt, mud, snot and everything else that Danny had collected over the past few hours. The lieutenant's hair was now a mess; and while he was far from the mess Danny was, he was now sharing the events of the afternoon. Stunned, the LT looked back and forth at Danny and his appearance. Before he could say anything, the EMTs came in and took one look at Danny and rolled in the gurney for transport. The LT was trying to put words together and maybe even yell at Danny but not with all the witnesses. Frustrated, he spun on his heal and announced to the dispatcher that he was heading home to get a shower and cleaned up.

For once the lieutenant was leaving the building, Danny thought. He wanted to say something, but right now, it all looked like bumping into the LT was an accident. He wanted to keep it that way.

Danny was checked out and cleaned up at the hospital and diagnosed with a possible mild concussion. He was given a note for five days of medical leave and instructed to be re-checked by his own doctor to be cleared for duty. When Danny did go back to work, the same dispatcher was on duty who was working the night of the fight. Danny asked, "Hey, when I called for help, what happened in here?"

"Nothing," said the dispatcher in a resigned voice.

"What do you mean nothing? Did you tell the lieutenant I was calling for help? I even hit the panic button on the portable. What did he do?" Danny wanted to know.

"I didn't have to tell him anything," was the quiet response. "He was standing right behind me and heard every word and heard all the noise and shouting in the background. He saw the officer-needs-assistance light and tone come on. He had me silence the tone."

"What did he do?"

"He said you were probably over reacting and got himself a coffee."

Danny was still flying up I-95 and Geri was listening to dead air on the phone. But the flashback blocked everything else out. He could not forget that day, ever. And the memories continued.

"Oh, and there is a note in your pigeon hole from the wife of the guy you almost shot. She has been coming in every day since the incident to see you but of course you were out on medical."

Sure, now I am going to get sued for excessive force. What else could go wrong? Danny opened the letter expecting the worst. As he read each line his expression became into one of complete disbelief.

The dispatcher saw the look and figured it was trouble. "Lawsuit time?"

The letter was in beautifully feminine flowing script.

Dear Officer Gilcrest, I want to thank you for not killing my husband the other day. With what he did you had every right to shoot him, but you didn't. I thank God every day that they sent you and not someone else who might have killed him. Billy has had a lot

51

of problems since returning from the Marines. A few beers and the wrong song or the offending word can set him off, and he is a different person. Right now, he is at the VA getting help, and I hope it works. The court is making his treatment mandatory; and if he doesn't follow through, he will be back in jail. I understand that you were also a Marine and spent time in the Middle East. Maybe you and Billy served together at some point? I wanted to tell you this in person, but I can't take too much time away from my job. I visit with Billy every day. I know your job is dangerous, and I will pray for you every day.

May the Lord protect you,

Emily

Danny carefully folded the letter and placed it in his notebook. He exchanged glances with the dispatcher, who stared back with questioning eyes. All Danny could say was, "Ya never know."

He had covered some distance on I-95 while recalling the incident. He was shaking his head as he relived the flashback of that night. It only took him a few seconds to fast forward through that night as the events screamed through his brain remembering every detail. He had forgotten that Geri was on the other end wondering about the dead air on the phone.

"Danny are you still there, hello, can you hear me?" Her voice brought him back to the present. He had travelled a mile of more without even remembering it.

"Oh yeah, I am back. My blood pressure just spiked, and my knuckles are turning white on the steering wheel. I was just recalling when Cornell almost got me killed. Going back to work for him will be a pleasure."

Then Geri was back. "I'm not trying to crank you up, but I thought you should know before you walked in on it and got surprised. Besides he is only there for a few months or so until the new chief can complete his prior contract. Then Cornell is out of the chief's position and back in patrol."

"Maybe I can take vacation for month and wait him out," said Danny. "How did they ever pick him?" he asked.

"Well," said Geri, "There are a couple of troopers who live in town, and they told me that the elected officials love him. Whatever they ask him to do, he does. He doesn't oppose anyone's suggestions and agrees to just about anything. They even proposed that the department staffing and non-traffic overtime be cut, and he is seeing what he can do to make that happen. They also suggested that more part-timers be brought on working just short of fulltime hours to cut down on the salaries and expenses."

This is a disaster, thought Danny. On the bright side, it was only temporary and maybe he would be gone before too much damage was done.

"I will call you when I am a few hours away from York Lake, and we can firm up a time when I will be there."

"Sounds good, but are you OK?"

Danny thought about what Geri had just told him and the changes at the department. He also flashed to his conversation with Tom Deverse and the potential for hard feelings in the department and the town. At least Geri and Bear would be on his side. When he got in the jeep at Quantico to head home, he thought he was coming back to a better department, a changed department. Well, it had changed; how much more damage could happen?

"Geri, I have to get back to concentrating on driving before I run off the road. I will call tomorrow and see you at the lake."

"Well, Jarhead, be careful and don't speed. You know what a bunch of pricks those state troopers can be."

"Yes, I do, young lady, yes I do."

"Bite me." And the phone went dead.

What a sweet delicate little thing she is, Danny thought, as he cranked up a Bruce Springsteen CD and headed up the highway back to Maidstone.

Chapter 9

Traffic through New Jersey and New York City was a nightmare. Lower Connecticut wasn't much better, but once he hit Bridgeport and got on Route 8 north, everything eased up. All the traffic was heading south, so it was smooth sailing. He wasn't disappointed. The dogwoods were out, and there was a magnificent view. It would have been quicker going up the New York Thruway, but it didn't have the rock ledges or the dogwood trees. The extra time was worth it. Danny needed to mellow out and prepare for the next few months. Seeing the Litchfield Hills and the Berkshires would help; and, of course, there were Geri and Bear. If he could just maintain a low profile and stay off anyone's shit list, he might make it until the new chief got sworn in. After what Deverse had told him, he knew that line of thinking wasn't even a possibility. He was forewarned. He had to be careful. He promised himself that he would not take undue risks. Danny vowed to maintain as low a profile as possible. Danny knew he was in trouble.

Danny stopped off at the Locker in Litchfield and the Smoke House in Goshen to pick up a few things for lunch and the days ahead. He could remember being in Iraq and Afghanistan and thinking of those special places in and near the Berkshires and hoping he would at some point get back there. Well he though, *I am not going to worry about what might happen. There are some very good things here in the hills, and I am going to enjoy them.* After a couple of more stops, Danny got to York Lake and began setting things up. The air was cool and the sky was blue; there were just enough white puffy clouds in the sky. To add to the perfection, there wasn't a mosquito anywhere. Everything was ready to go, and he had some time to pass before Geri arrived with Bear. He grabbed one of the sports drinks from the cooler and poured a few ounces of Pinot Grigio into his cup. Knowing that the park rangers might be around, Danny had transferred the wine into the sports drink bottles. Alcohol was not permitted at the park, but sports drinks were just fine. He understood the rules and the reason for the rules. He wasn't about to be chugging beer and smashing bottles in the fireplace. He was not going to pull rank on the ranger or have Geri pull out her state police shield. That would have definitely trumped the ranger, but it was chicken-shit. The ranger would have just been doing his job and didn't need that kind of crap or disrespect. Even though they were cops, they should show more class than to flaunt it in the ranger's face. Low profile at all times.

Geri arrived, and fortunately Bear came running when he saw Danny. Geri moved slower giving Bear and Danny their moment; but when she closed in, Danny was all hers. The embrace was just short of crushing. Bear stood by waiting to get back into the action, not liking the fact that he was not the center of attention. Being left out Bear began to notice all the good smells coming from the picnic table and began to check things out. Before lunch disappeared, Geri noticed Bear's undivided attention to what was on the table.

"Hey, buddy; back off if you know what's good for you."

Bear gave her a sideways glance, but moved back from the table in slow motion.

"It seems Bear knows who the boss is. I hope he hasn't forgotten who I am," said Danny.

"We have been very close over the past two plus months, but I am sure he knows who you are. We just need to properly establish the pecking order."

"That does not sound good."

"It could be worse; we could be talking about what a great guy you were and how much we miss you."

"Good point; I will try to fit in."

They sat at the lake looking over the absolutely flat water reflecting all the trees. They sampled the items from the Locker and the Smoke House, and Geri never even questioned the sports bottle wine. They sat there for a long time admiring the view not saying a word. Eventually the sun started to sink low in the sky, and Danny broke the silence.

"It is going to be very strange going back. The last time I was in the station, I signed out with the cruiser that night. After almost getting shot, I spoke briefly with Gary Carlson. Then I was in the FBI car on the way out of town. I didn't even pack my own bag. The FBI picked up the Jeep and brought it down to Quantico. One minute I was there and the next south bound. Now after two and a half months, I am coming back; and for the most part everything is now history. It is going to be strange getting back in a cruiser and driving around town."

Danny went on to explain what Agent Deverse had told him about the investigation and some of the feelings the people in town had toward him. Agent Deverse would be his FBI contact for the near term. Now he had to work for Lieutenant/Chief Cornell.

"He was bad enough as a lieutenant; but now as chief with final authority, this could be the end of the line for me."

"Well, he might be too busy to bother with you. Remember that piece of property his family had up on the hill behind the marsh area off of East Lake Road?"

"Oh, yes, I remember it well. It was a great place with all the duck hunters. But you couldn't get to it for all the wetlands you had to cross, and then the one location that would be perfect for a house was close to two thousand feet or more off the road. He doesn't have the kind of money to put in a road that long or that detailed. Hell, he doesn't have the bucks to build any house with his two divorces. There would be planning and zoning and inland/wetlands. The town fathers would never go for it; and even if they did, it would take forever to get all the approvals and permits. The attorney fees would kill him."

"Well, not to ruin a perfect lunch at a beautiful lake, but the road into the property is currently under construction. The site location is all marked out, and it looks like they will start construction in the next month or so."

Danny stared at her like she had two heads or maybe way too much wine. Looking at her serious face, he knew she wasn't making this up.

"How in the world is this possible? When I went to Quantico, he was living in a one-bedroom condo. The rumor was that he was having trouble with the association fees. He even started a petition to stop the roof replacements on the condos that were twenty-five years old. He couldn't afford the assessment they were going to put on the unit owners. I can only guess what a house on the hill overlooking the marsh is going to cost. It is a beautiful location, but where is he getting that kind of money? Did someone die that I don't know about and leave him some huge bucks?"

Geri gave him a serious look and then proceeded.

"To my knowledge, no one died; but all of a sudden he has a whole bunch of low-life friends in high or influential positions. You will never guess who is one of his morning coffee buddies."

"Cornell never goes out for coffee. He is too cheap and only drinks the department coffee. He pays his five bucks a month and drinks twenty dollars' worth."

"Does the name Quentin Worthington ring a bell?"

Danny was floored. For several seconds he just stammered away not saying a full sentence or even a complete word.

"Brad's dad? No way. You're telling me that Brad kills Penny, and Lieutenant Snyder covers it up. The money for the cover-up is rumored to come from Quentin, but so far there hasn't been a direct connection. Either way, the PD has locked up Brad. He is now going to do some serious time, and Quentin is being buddy-buddy with the new chief? There is something seriously wrong with this picture."

"They appear to be best of friends and see each other every day at the coffee shop. Now there are all those connections that Quentin has."

"I know about some, but there are so many it's hard to keep track. There is the wife and her brother who works for the state. His wife is on town boards--there are just so many of them it gets confusing. The fact that they have different last names but are all related somehow hides the connections."

"Exactly true, and that is how he got approval so quickly. It was a done deal before it went before the commission. The brother-in-law's wife saw that the road was approved without so much as one objection or impact review."

"But where is the money coming from? Who is paying for the road and the house? If he can't afford a one-bedroom condo, how is he pulling this off?" Danny heard everything but still did not believe it.

"That," said Geri "is the question. No one knows. We thought it might be a second attempt to bag the case, but there have not been any moves in that direction. The case against Brad, or should I say the defense, is moving toward guilty by reason of insanity. With the help of his cupcake shrink new girlfriend, Brad just might pull it off."

Danny though back to the night of the murder and the events that followed. Brad met this drop-dead gorgeous psychologist in the ER. She was there to help him through his wife's tragic suicide. During the course of the suicide, really a murder, good ole Brad nearly blew his hand off. Lieutenant Snyder stepped in and bagged the case, and Brad got probation. It should have been fifteen to life, but the lieutenant took care of that.

"Now how is she going to convince a jury that her current boyfriend was nuts at the time of the murder?"

"She isn't," said Geri, "but she has convinced several associates that he was insane at the time he pulled the trigger. They are supporting her theory."

"OK, that's crazy, and I don't think it will fly. But how does that get Cornell and Quentin together? He wasn't there and, as usual, never left the building so he can't testify to anything that happened that night."

"No idea, but way off the record because I have been told to stay out of this. The state and the feds are looking at Quentin, and I have no idea why unless it is about the payoff to Snyder."

"The feds as in the FBI?" Danny asked.

"They are in the office, and I do see them. The IRS is in the office more than the FBI. The Organized Crime Task Force is very compartmentalized for good reason. I am assigned to

OCTF, but not that squad. As I said, they don't want me in on this. I am only getting bits of information here and there from conversations that I overhear or emails that come across my desk. The thing is I am not getting the feeling that they are on to something and ready to move in. They are digging, but no one gives the impression that they have a lock on something or that arrests are about to go down. You know the look of confidence cops get when they are putting the pieces together and things are falling into place? There have not been any of those looks. There isn't anyone with a smile on their face or sure of themselves attitude when they come out of a meeting. They all look determined, but frustrated. Something is going on. Cornell is all of a sudden financially well off and has a new friend that should hate the police department. There is a connection there--I just don't know what it is."

"And me, Danny the Boy Scout Gilcrest, who has pissed off both of them, will be walking right into the middle of whatever this is."

Chapter 10

Danny and Geri sat at the lake for several more hours not saying much. Both were deep in thought. The lake was beautiful, but they hardly noticed. Bear was fine with everything. From time to time some cheese or smoked meat would come his way; for him, life was good. Geri was trying to figure out what was really going on with the case or how she could get more information and not get fired. Danny was considering his future and trying to understand how two very different people had now become close friends. There was the sudden windfall of cash for Lincoln Cornell to build a house with access through a swamp. There was the expedited zoning meeting by the wetlands commission to approve building a road through a centuries-old marsh. In past town hall meetings, developers took years to get approval to make any changes to designated wetlands areas. This time, it sounds as if it were a done deal before they walked in the door. None of this had been in the works three months ago; and in the blink of an eye, things had changed.

The sun was getting low when Geri announced, "I would like to stay here the rest of the night, but I have to go to work tomorrow and drive all the way back to Fort Devens. You have to report in tomorrow and get cleared for duty so we should pack things up and get on the road."

"You are right, but you know what I really need?"

Geri had an idea what that would be and gave him a quick smile. She had hoped that Danny would be interested in other things beyond the political climate in Maidstone. "What might that be?" The answer wasn't the one she was looking for.

"A quarter of a million dollars in uncut diamonds."

"Say what?"

"If I had the diamonds, I wouldn't have to go back to work." At this point Danny realized he had screwed up big time and had come up with the wrong answer. The look on Geri's face was not one of hurt. It was one that conveyed a potential for a severe beating at the hands of one pissed-off young lady. "Sorry. I just keep thinking about the shit-storm I have to face, and I am having trouble thinking of anything else."

"Start thinking of something else, or Bear and I are outta here."

"Would a back rub be in order?"

"You bet a back rub is in order, and it better be a long, slow back rub--and you don't stop until I tell you. Got it?"

"Yes ma'am. Let's pack it up and head out."

They gathered everything, loaded Bear in the Jeep, and headed for Maidstone. It would be good to get back to the barn with Geri there. It would be a good welcome home. The barn was more than just a barn but a nicely furnished apartment on a sprawling estate. So far it was good to be back, but who knew what the future held for Danny. These new developments and the information from Agent Deverse gave Danny a lot to think about. How could a quiet little town in the Berkshires have so many problems? Danny had spent the first eighteen years of his life in these hills and never had any idea about what was going on.

Chapter 11

After a wonderful night in the barn, it was back to the PD to check in. There was the mandatory appointment with the doctor to be cleared to return to duty. Danny was concerned about his return to the police station, but once inside the apprehension melted away. The entire department had turned out to greet him, and there were handshakes and bear hugs all around. There was a cake and sparkling cider to toast the occasion. Danny was presented with a fake bill for the shotgun-blasted door and a bag full of broken glass from the window. Even the acting chief was there. He made his way through the throng of officers and staff, took Danny's hand, and welcomed him back. It was not an honest grip. No one could hear the words, and the greeting had no indication of sincerity. It was a required formality that had to be done but with absolutely no conviction. It lasted for only the briefest of a few seconds, and the chief retreated down the hall back to his office. If anyone noticed, there was no indication of the abbreviated welcome home from the boss. People were more intent on their own greetings.

The chief's quick passing gave others a better opportunity to speak with Danny. For the returning hero, the mandatory welcome home from his new boss spoke volumes. Yes, he had been greeted and welcomed home. Yes, all the right words were said. Yes, the chief made it a point of being seen by all the members of the department. But the grip, the limited eye contact, the rehearsed "welcome home" told it all. The immediate disappearing act sealed it. Danny was not invited back to the chief's office to ask how he was doing or how the academy had been. There were no questions or comments about Danny's future. Danny had never been on good terms with the acting chief. Now Danny's new boss was friends with the father of a mutt Danny was responsible for sending to prison for a very long time. The acting chief's new-found friend was also under investigation for funding the cover-up. Things were not looking good from where Danny stood. Everyone else was glad to see him, and Danny was soon lost in the noise and questions.

It seemed like only a few minutes, but the greetings and conversation went on for over an hour. Phones had to be answered, radio calls needed response, so people drifted away back to work. Finally, it was just Danny and Gary Carlson the last Maidstone officer to see Danny after the shooting. There were a few other people having side conversations in the break room.

"Let's hit the locker room," said Danny. "I have to see what I need to bring in and what I need to clean up."

Gary was about to say something when Danny noticed changes in the department. "Hey, are those new computers and screens in there?"

"Oh, yes," said Gary, "new computers and new radios."

"How did the department come up with that kind of money so quick? None of this was in the pipeline when I left."

"There was a federal grant that came through to test out some new equipment and software," said Gary. "The Western Regional Law Enforcement Planning Committee thought we could use the equipment after our comms failed so many times."

"This must have cost a fortune."

"No idea, I have never seen the bill."

They made their way into the locker room, and Danny stopped in front of his locker. His name had been removed, and the lock on the handle was missing. Danny stared at the handle and then at the adhesive residue on the door where his name plate had been. He looked at the door and then at Gary trying to find the words. Gary spoke first.

"I was going to tell you; but with all the commotion and stuff, I never got the chance."

"What the hell is going on, who went into my locker?"

"Everything was fine," began Gary. "After Cornell was made acting chief, he had detectives come down and cut the lock. He stood by and watched the entire time and had the inventory videoed. Each and every item was removed and cataloged. He even had the numbers on your summons book copied. It took a couple of hours."

Danny opened his locker. There was nothing inside.

"So where is all of my gear?"

"It is being held in the evidence vault," was the almost-whispered reply.

"Am I in trouble? Do I need a lawyer?" asked Danny staring into the empty locker.

"They didn't find one thing, and that did not make Cornell all that happy. When the detectives were done and Cornell saw that they hadn't found anything, he just grunted and walked away in a huff. The detectives said they were shittin themselves afraid of what they might find. When they came up with zip, they were relieved to tell Cornell. They thought he would be pleased. Instead they got a completely opposite reaction. At that point it dawned on them that they were supposed to find something. In any other locker they might have found some dope that had been seized or maybe a weapon that wasn't supposed to be there or say maybe some porn." Trying to lighten things up, Gary added, "They did find a dirty shirt they could pin on you."

Danny's mind was racing. Deverse was right and things were not looking good. He was going to have to watch his back every second from now on. Everything he did was going to be under a microscope. One miss-step, one beer too many, one cross word to a citizen could cost him his job.

Danny made his way up to the Detective Division and approached the sergeant who was acting as the supervising detective lieutenant until one could be promoted. The sergeant was genuinely glad to see Danny and had been there for the welcome home get-together. He stood when Danny came in and pumped his hand right up until Danny asked for his gear. The color drained from the sergeant's face, and he sank back into his chair and motioned for Danny to sit. He gazed at Danny for a minute then realized the door was still open. He quickly got up and closed the door ever so quietly.

"Danny," he began, "it wasn't my idea. The word came down to inventory your gear and that you might not be coming back. I was told that we had to video the whole thing. I'm sorry; it wasn't my idea."

"So, can I get my gear back?"

The sergeant nodded his head and led Danny to the evidence vault. As they were going through the inventory, Danny heard footsteps behind him and turned to see Cornell glaring at him.

"I hope it's all there," stated the acting chief.

"I am sure it all is," countered Danny. "These guys are all cops and can be trusted."

The chief's face went red. Danny couldn't figure if it were embarrassment, anger, or something else. Maybe it was several things. *Well*, thought Danny, *he knows that I know, and I know I have to watch my step. How do you fight your own team and expect to win?* However this turned out, it didn't look good for Danny. Every item was there, and each had been neatly placed in storage with the dirty shirt folded as thought it had just come from the cleaners. The detectives might have searched his locker, but they had treated his gear with respect.

As Danny exited the police department, he had more on his mind than he could process. That was when his cell phone rang. He checked the number and was about to silence the call when he saw that the prefix was from Virginia.

"Hello," was all Danny said.

The voice on the other end was equally as brief. "Do you know who this is?"

It was the voice of Agent Tom Deverse. Danny knew they would be talking, but he never expected it would be this soon. "Yes, I do."

"Good. There is a package waiting for you at your post office box down in Great Barrington."

"I don't have a post office box in Great Barrington," was the annoyed response.

"Yes, you do. The number is 1249 and the code is A-J-K. There is a package there waiting for you. Do not tell anyone you have it, not even Geri. Never use it at home, in your Jeep, at the station, or in a cruiser. If you do use it on duty, walk away from the patrol vehicle and leave your portable radio in the vehicle."

"We need to talk," stated Danny.

"Yes, we do, but not on this phone. Go check your PO Box." The call ended.

Danny stared at the phone for a second, tempted to call Deverse back and ask him what the hell was going on. He then quickly looked around. In a smooth motion put his cell phone back in his pocket and made his way to the Jeep. He made the short trip to Great Barrington, and after several tries, he got the post office box open. He took the package and headed out the door. It was a nice day, so he made his way to the town green. Danny found a shady spot on a bench away from everyone. He opened the package, and there was a new cell phone and charger. He was going to call Deverse and then realized he didn't have his number. He was about to go back to the Jeep and check the number on his cell phone. Instead he looked at the numbers in the phone. As he suspected, there was a number and only one number in the directory. He punched the send key. The call was answered in just a few rings.

"How do you like your early Christmas present," Deverse wanted to know.

"How did you know I would need it?"

"Do you need it?"

"I am pretty sure I am going to need a lot more than a cell phone."

"This is just a start. Now a few things about the phone. If you hit the side button once, it lights up the screen. Hit that button twice and nothing happens. That is just in case your fat fingers stutter. Now hit the button three times, and the phone begins recording. It will keep recording until you hit the button three more times. Now for the James Bond stuff. Hit the button three times and then pause. Then hold the button down for a few seconds. The phone will transmit all data to a receiver and store it. Once the dump is complete, the phone will then have a battery fire, so don't put it in your pocket."

"I will try and remember all this. Do you think I will need to destroy the phone?"

"Probably not. But it is always good to have that option, just in case."

"How was your welcome home?"

"Great, as long as you don't include the acting chief. I thought there might be problems, but I had no idea it would be like this."

"Any hints from anyone else who might not be happy to see you?"

"Not that I could detect, but the one guy in that position is more than enough to make my life miserable. He can direct others to do his bidding."

"Call this number back after you get your thoughts collected and leave a detailed voice message about what happened today. Any time you think something important happened, do the same. If you need to talk to me, call, hang up, and then call right back. I should pick up unless I am in the shower or getting lucky."

"When was the last time you got lucky?"

"I am in the shower a lot."

"Again, how did you know I would need this phone?"

"Good guess."

"Bullshit."

"Correct."

"Am I now working for the feds?"

"Sort of."

"Are you paying me?"

"Probably not but we will do our best to make sure you don't get fired. We are going to take care of you."

"Like the last time when I almost got blown in half taken care of?"

"Ouch. I promise we will do better this time."

"The check is in the mail, and you will respect me in the morning?"

Deverse gave a big sigh. "Something like that, but better. You need us. Besides Geri and Bear, we are the only true friends for sure that you have." The line went dead.

Danny pocketed the phone and headed back to Maidstone. Right now, Baghdad made more sense than Maidstone.

Chapter 12

Danny had a lot to think about on the ride back. He had been assigned to midnights. While some though it was a slap in the face, Danny looked forward to it. He never slept on the job. Being down there in the dark working midnights would keep some distance between him and Cornell. As a lieutenant in patrol, Cornell almost always managed not to work on the midnight shift even when he was assigned. He would use his vacation and sick time to miss work. Whenever possible, he would try for an assignment or training during his midnight shift tours. Cornell was not known for late nights or even early mornings so the midnight shift would be a nice quiet place for Danny.

Danny made some quick notes about the day's events. He then made his first report to the FBI. His thoughts drifted as to what he was doing. Was he now an informant, a snitch, an undercover operative, or just maybe a sitting duck being used as bait? Danny wanted to keep his notes, but he also knew that at any time he could misplace them, or they could somehow fall into the wrong hands. He tore the notes into little pieces and then mixed them in with what was left of a cup of coffee. He put them in one of the street side trash cans right on Main Street. Even if someone watched him dump the coffee cup, no one would give it a second thought. He couldn't see a person going through the trash on Main Street.

If they did and happened to find the right coffee cup, it wouldn't do them any good.

Danny started his first midnight shift with a whole new attitude and a different perspective. He was very surprised when he spotted the chief's cruiser out in town well after midnight. Cornell was never known to leave the station, and late-night random drives through town were not something he ever did. Danny had no doubt that he was being watched and watched very closely. He had never gone in the hole like some of the officers. Going in the hole would entail finding a very secluded spot off the beaten path to catch a few hours of sleep. If asked, the officers would claim they were stopped writing a report. Danny's tactic was more Marine Corps style. He would find a perch—a place where he could see all around and no one could sneak up on him without that person being observed. Most of the time it would be with the headlights and running lights on so that he could be seen and act as a deterrent. Other times when he wanted to see and not be seen, he would find a perch with a good field of view. He would then turn off all of his lights in a spot that created a black hole that the street lights would not illuminate. He would be in plain sight if a person approached and got behind the glare of the lights. He didn't care if anyone found him--not even the chief--because he was never asleep or doing anything wrong. After several futile attempts to catch Danny screwing off, Cornell couldn't keep up with the late hours and gave up. He went back to his old routine. A quick pass by Cornell's condo would confirm that his personal vehicle and the cruiser were there. The acting chief was in for the night.

Now Danny had always been on the lookout for things that were out of place when on patrol. He would be looking for those small things that would be considered abnormal, activities that didn't fit in to the normal routine of Maidstone.

But something was going on in town, and it was not coming across as unusual or strange. Whatever it was fit in and did not stand out. It was like Danny and his blacked-out perch: there in plain sight but invisible. Danny had his work cut out for him. With Cornell tucked in bed, he had no distractions. Now it was time to get to work.

Chapter 13

First chance Danny got, he swung down to the new Cornell homestead that was under construction. For someone with no visible extra cash, there was an awful lot of equipment parked at the job site. There was a backhoe, heavy duty loader, a dump truck, a large fork lift, a foundation truck, and a couple of mobile storage containers. There was also lots of other equipment and job-boxes. Just having this amount of money in equipment parked did not sound cost effective, but here it was.

Danny wrote down every contractor name on the vehicles and took down all the registration numbers that he could find. Only one vehicle bore the Worthington name. He had to do some research, but couldn't use the department computers. Online databases sometimes have tracking and report to the people who are being searched. *There's gotta be a way*, Danny thought. *I really don't want to count on the FBI. Deverse is a nice guy, but he holds things back. I could stumble on some good leads and bring them to the FBI. They in turn would nod their heads and not tell me where they led. Think, Jarhead, and with that the light bulb went on.*

Next day when off duty, Danny made his way down to the beautiful old town of Litchfield, Connecticut. He found himself standing in front of the library wondering *okay, I am here; now what? If you are old school and doing research, you go to*

the library. Well, I am here; I guess it would help if I went inside.
Danny spotted a young lady behind the counter and asked to sign on to one of the computers.

"Of course, take your pick. No one has signed on yet this morning," was the smiling reply.

She was a lovely young lady about Danny's age, and she had dark hair and those nerdy glasses that actually made her look very sexy. Her blouse was also buttoned a bit low, but Danny wasn't complaining. As his thoughts came together, he made a quick look around to see if Geri were there. He then made a second slower scan to see just who was there. Being the middle of the morning during the week, the place was almost deserted. No one was paying any attention to him.

Danny wondered if he were being paranoid. No, he concluded, and realized that he was just being cautious. As Danny pondered the past, he looked at the computer trying to figure out where to start. He didn't want to leave a trail, but he had to get some answers before he did something to get himself jammed up. The librarian had been watching Danny looking intently at the computer and decided to help.

"You do know how to use a computer?" she asked. "You look intimidated."

Danny snapped out of his thoughts embarrassed that she would be posing that question to him. Did he really look that dumb? "No, I am just trying to figure out where to start."

"Well, what is it that you are trying to do?"

Now Danny knew exactly what he wanted to do but was not about to share with her or anyone else for that matter. Only now he had to think fast. She had asked a reasonable question. There should be an easy and quick explanation. "Well, ya know, ya see, it's like this," and Danny stumbled trying to find a good and believable reason for doing research on people. "I am trying to find guys I served with in the Marines, and I am not sure how to go about it."

"That is fairly easy. There are several databases with that kind of information. It will cost you a few bucks, and you need some personal information like the hometown, date of birth, or a social security number."

Now if Danny was really trying to find his buddie, it would have been easy. He had all that information and even hometown addresses. Unfortunately, he had to wing it because he was trying to cover his tracks. "I don't have all that much information. I would like to locate about 250 guys. I really don't have that kind of money to do that many paid searches."

"There are a lot of free public records that you can search. If you have a name and a state, you can start there. If you have more information, you can make the search narrower; and it will go a lot quicker. There are newspaper articles about guys going into and coming out of the service. There are weddings, birth announcements, tax records, court filings, even court cases. There are all kinds of places where there is a chance for a name association. There are the obituary columns that list lots of relatives to whomever passed. I hope you don't find any of your friends in there, but maybe they will be listed as a relative. It is a lot more work than going to the paid sites, but it still gets the job done. There is a ton of information out there on the internet."

Now Danny had a course of action, and he was ready to move....but the librarian was still hanging in there ready to help, or maybe help herself.

"Thanks, let me give it a shot. If I run into trouble or get bogged down and need some more guidance, I will give you a holler." She wasn't taking the hint. "Please, I am intimidated enough by the computer and typing with both fingers. If you watch me, I will really screw this up."

With a very nice smile, she turned away. Over her shoulder she gave a parting word, "Anything you need help with, anytime, I will be right over."

Danny gave a big sigh, and Geri flashed in his mind. Don't screw this up, he thought, the search or Geri. He got to work. It started off slow until he got the hang of it. Then it was page after page of related information. He could not believe the details he was coming up with or the interwoven picture it was painting of the Quentin Worthington family and their associates. He had started with the names and addresses on the trucks and then the names he knew that were close in the Worthington family. His search went back to Quentin's great, great grandfather, Bradford Covington Worthington. Old Covington was a good Swamp Yankee and had nine kids, seven who made it to adulthood. Three were girls. That is where the family name in some respects gets lost but expands the family. While the marriages of the girls changed the name, it did not change the clan mentality of the family. This continued on for the next three generations making an ever-expanding circle. The search could not consider the people not directly related to the family, but who became close associates through friendship, business deals, affairs, and gay associations. Danny was having a hard time keeping track of the names and down loaded them to a flash drive. There was a tap on his shoulder, and he almost jumped out of the chair.

"Sorry, I hope I didn't scare you, but I wanted to let you know I was leaving." It was the librarian, and she was going to give it one more shot. She had a somewhat sly smile on her face. "Here," and she handed Danny a piece of paper with a number written on it. "In case you run into trouble or anything else comes to mind, give me a call." With that she rubbed his shoulder and headed for the door ever so slowly.

Focus, Danny boy, focus, he thought; and she was gone. Danny's brain was full and then the interruption. However nice, it had altered his train of thought and where he was going. He had so much information that it was hard to keep it straight. Granted Covington and the next generation were all dead, but that marriage started an inverse pyramid that made the Quentin Worthington family huge. That marriage and others had generated more than thirty-five grandchildren. And the next generation was even bigger. The marriages also meant that the new spouses brought their families into the clan that Danny was now referring to as the Quentin Worthington group. The bottom line was that every truck and labeled piece of equipment at Cornell's jobsite had a direct or just slightly indirect connection to Quentin. Why in the world would Quentin want to be the big favor guy with Cornell unless there were plans to make sure the new chief never showed up? Was there some way Cornell would get the job? Even then what could Cornell do that Quentin would be his major benefactor? Danny had information and lots of questions, and he wanted to share it with Deverse. What would he get in return from the FBI? If he had found this much information, why hadn't the FBI? He now had lots of answers but created more questions.

Danny went to the Litchfield town green and bought a coffee. He found a park bench in the shade and made a call using the special cell phone. The call wasn't long as he could not remember and link specific details in a perfect order. He did explain going all the way back to Covington, how the Worthington clan enlarged and spread out all through the Berkshires, Western Massachusetts and into New York and Vermont.

After the first call, he made a second call to the same number--this time with the quick hang up to trigger a return call from Deverse. He didn't have long to wait.

"Yo, Danny boy, what's up?" Deverse wanted to know.

"I have been doing some research. I left a message before, but there are just too many details to leave it in a recording."

"You weren't using yours or department's equipment, I hope."

"No, I hit the library down in Litchfield. I checked the place out when I went in, and there wasn't anyone there that I recognized. Heck, there was hardly anyone there."

"What did you come up with that will help?"

"I went back like five generations of the Worthington clan and came up with some very interesting connections all over a big area of Western Massachusetts and the nearby states." Danny went on to explain all the names and connections as best he could remember, hitting the real powers that controlled things in the Worthington Clan and, in turn, things in the Berkshires. "I came up with no less than 492 people related to or closely associated with the Worthington Clan."

"Danny, we can't run down that many people. Is there a way of culling some of them out?"

"Oh, they have culled themselves, so to speak. The history I found goes back into the 1800s, so a whole bunch of them are dead. The kicker is that you have to look back that far to see the associations today. This all started back around the Civil War. Right now, I have 168 blood relatives still alive, and most live within a one-hundred-mile radius of Maidstone with the largest percentage being less than fifty miles away. But the background shows the connections that you wouldn't see because the names are not always Worthington. There is a senator, one congressman, two state legislators, one governor back in the early 1900s, all kinds of commissioners and public servants along with a few lawyers, real estate brokers and presidents or CEOs of major companies in Western Mass. There are a lot of connections and influence coming from that family."

"Do any of the names stand out?" Deverse wanted to know.

"Most of them," was the short reply. "The kicker is there might be some people working for the FBI or the justice department that are part of or associated with the Worthington Clan. The name changes by marriage and the business connections get confusing and are open to interpretation. You might have people working on this who are playing for the other team. They might not be corrupt, but they could be doing the so-called favor and unknowingly sharing information."

"There are only a very limited number of agents on this from the FBI, but we have other agencies involved as well," said Deverse. "There is the support staff, the clerks, technicians and others who have some access. The other agencies have their people as well. I have to look into this and get back to you. How do you have the information stored?"

"It is stored on a flash drive," said Danny. "To make sure no one can scan it, I have the drive surrounded by metal and it's in a container that no one will ever check."

"Make a copy and I will arrange a meeting. Litchfield sounds like a good place, and we can talk more. I don't like the idea of having you hold copies of anything. From what you described, you're going to have to store it somehow. See you soon," and Deverse clicked off.

Chapter 14

"Ok, what have ya got?" Deverse cut straight to the chase without any fanfare or greeting.

"Oh no--first things first." Danny had his priorities, and when in Litchfield that meant two sugar cookies and a chocolate chip cookie with a medium coffee from the shop just off the green. Deverse relented, and the coffee, if not the cookies, sounded like a good start. They made their purchases and found a bench off to one side away from all the foot traffic on the south side of the green where all the shops were located. Danny put his coffee down and reached into his left pocket and retrieved a Glock 17 9mm magazine. This caught Deverse off guard, and he watched Danny's right hand to see if it were going to move towards the small of his back where he knew Danny holstered his pistol. Deverse was wondering what had gone wrong. What in the world did Danny have in mind pulling a magazine out on the town green? Before Deverse could react or even ask a question, Danny sat down and began fiddling with the bottom plate on the magazine. He slid the plate off, and a wad of aluminum foil appeared. With Deverse looking on intently, Danny unwrapped the aluminum foil and produced a flash drive. He handed it to Deverse.

"It's all there. It isn't in a compiled order of any kind just the information that I found in the order I found it. I would really need a place to work on this with a big screen monitor and a printer. Just trying to organize things will be a nightmare. There is just so much information that I need to put it all together to take out the parts that don't matter. I can't really say they don't matter because they do have an association. Having said that, I still need those parts to put the links together, if only to eliminate them. Even if they are not direct players, just connections, it still has meaning. I have been thinking about the possibility that there might be someone on the inside working for the other team. Most of the support staff would be hired from the local area, correct?"

"Yes, that is true. The lower paying jobs of the support staff and the non-technical jobs usually come from the local population. Because it could require moving, you don't see transfers in those areas until they become supervisors."

"Now some agents--not all--work their entire careers trying to get back to the place they call home. Some are immediately successful as they ask for one of the major cities close to where they grew up. Others from more rural areas try for someplace close or put in for assignments that would bring them closer to where they call home."

Deverse nodded his head in agreement. "You know there is more than one agency in on this investigation. We have only two from the FBI, and they are only part time. This isn't their focus. With so little information coming in, there isn't enough to keep them busy fulltime. I am not even sure about the staffing of the other agencies or how they are manning the unit or how much time they are devoting. Every federal agency likes to know it has a winner before starting or committing funds and resources. I have to guess that this isn't a priority. It was a priority when the bureau thought they had a wide-ranging case. They got Snyder, only to find a bunch of people who looked the other way."

Danny began to see Maidstone and the Worthington clan slipping so far onto the back burner that it was never going to happen.

"You have developed some great information, but right now it isn't taking us anywhere. We need a crime; that would really help. All we have are suspects we think are doing something illegal, but we don't know what. There is a lot of money moving around up here that isn't accounted for, but we cannot prove that anyone came by it illegally. Are you following me?"

Slowly Danny nodded his head. He came to the realization that he done a great job making connections but without identifying the crime.

"It's not over, just look at everything that has been uncovered. We knew the mob boys from New York had something going with Detective Lieutenant Snyder. We just couldn't make the solid connection until you came along. When they tried to make hits on you, Geri, and District Attorney Cohen, we got a home run. Sorry it almost got you killed. I know that sounds pretty lame, but the people running the operation up here thought they had it locked down. Who could predict that the hit team would change their plans and move everything up a few days?"

Danny was tired of hearing the same excuse, and it wasn't going to change anything no matter how often the feds apologized.

Deverse went on. "In the follow up, we know how much Snyder got paid to bag the case. We did financials on all the major players, and not one of them showed major transactions after the murder that couldn't be explained. We couldn't check everyone--just the people we could link to the case, like Brad's father. We were certain that he made the payoff, but there was no evidence. I guess it is possible that he kept two hundred and fifty thousand hidden in the mattress, but that doesn't seem likely. The accountants did find transactions and things that were strange, but could only justify the broad statement that something was wrong. But they couldn't say what was wrong. The trucking company just seems to be doing way better than it should be. Quenton Worthington might not have had anything to do with your attempted murder, but maybe he did have something to do with the cover up. We just can't make the connection. Snyder only talked with Quenton once, and that was the night of the murder. Even Snyder admits that he isn't sure where the money came from. The night of the murder, Snyder left the scene and called Quenton and told him what had gone down. He stated in no uncertain terms that Brad had pinned Penny to the wall and blew here brains out with a 10-gauge shotgun."

"Why doesn't he think the money came from Quenton?"

"Snyder's conversation with Quenton was short and one sided with Snyder doing most of the talking. When we interviewed Snyder, he tried to remember the exact words. Snyder's quote said it was something like, *that dumb son-of-a-bitch is going to pay for this. I will take care of him.* Snyder thought he meant that he was going to protect Brad and take care of him that way. But Quenton never called back to make any arrangements so Snyder sat on things for few days. Snyder then gets a FEDEX package with twenty-five thousand dollars and a typed note. The note stated that this was a first installment to make this go away. More cash would be coming as long as things were working out for Brad. If Brad can get away with no jail time, then Snyder would see a total of two hundred and fifty thousand dollars at the end of the trial. Snyder assumed it was all from Quenton. He couldn't think of anyone else in the family with that kind of cash available. Plus, Quenton was the only one he contacted."

"So, Danny, the case was bought and paid for, but we don't know by whom. We have a business that has more funds coming in than can be accounted for, but the accountants at the bureau can't figure it out. No one is getting results so the brass in DC are pulling the agents from the active investigation. They are leaving me, but you are only a small part of my assignments. This is all up to you, Danny boy."

"Are you telling me the FBI thinks that a rookie small town cop can put this together when the mighty FBI with all their resources struck out?"

"Yes."

That was not the answer Danny expected, but it was the one he got.

"Danny," Deverse said as he began to leave. "This is your town. You know something is wrong when you see it. You know when something just doesn't fit because you know what you are supposed to be seeing. An outsider does not have your perspective. Look, listen, think, be patient, and at some point, you will figure it out. You know the players and the connections. You have come up with associations that you weren't aware of. See what connects. I will help where I can. If you get something going, then I can get this investigation turned back on. The big boys in DC were ecstatic with the take down of all those mob guys from New York City and Albany. Their interest was piqued when it looked like more cases were coming our way. Now that it isn't a slam dunk, they are ready to move on."

"I am not feeling the love. This is starting to feel like a snowy night in February, and I am all alone again. This time, I have a chief of police who is after me for god only knows what. His new best friend is the father of a guy I am helping to put away for a long time."

"I know what you are saying, but you have to trust me on this. Chief Cornell will never be able to touch you unless you do something really stupid. Don't get drunk. Don't date a stripper. Don't hit anyone who doesn't deserve it and remain professional."

"Is this one more of those, *the FBI is not at liberty to comment on this?*"

"You do learn quickly. Just be professional, and he can't touch you. He doesn't know it; but if he makes a move on you, there will be a phone call. That's all I can say. Get back to work."

They shook hands and departed with Deverse wondering if he had said too much. Danny was wondering where to go from here.

Chapter 15

Life on the midnight shift in early spring remained quiet. The summer people had not yet arrived, and the ski season was long over. Soon the concerts at Tanglewood would start up along with all the other attractions in and around Maidstone. Inns and quest houses would fill up. Main Street would be a flurry of traffic and pedestrians. Danny was still at a loss for what to do. His concern wasn't only for the ongoing investigation but also for his life. With Cornell the chief, Danny was always looking over his shoulder. He was conscious of every decision or action. The constant second guessing and Monday morning quarterbacking was taking a toll. The midnight shift almost demanded that an officer go looking for something rather than waiting for it to happen. Laying low was easy; but by the same token, Danny had to show activity. If he didn't make stops, write tickets, or respond to calls, his activity sheet would look like he didn't do anything all night. So, Danny would make a few motor vehicle stops every night. Verbal or written warnings were the norm. He didn't like writing a summons unless he had a real violator. This gave Danny lots of time to think about Brad and Brad's father, old man Quenton Worthington.

Danny was in his favorite perch on Main Street where he could see almost all of the commercial operations in town. But he wasn't the only one parked there. A short distance down the road, a tractor trailer oil truck was parked idling away. There was no reason for it to be there this time of night. Even during the day, it would be unusual because there was no place to make that size delivery. *Maybe he is having some sort of mechanical problem,* thought Danny; and he decided to check it out. If nothing else, the neighbors would at some point complain about an idling truck outside their window.

Danny startled the driver. "Good evening. Are you having trouble with the rig?"

The truck driver was surprised to see a police officer, but at the same time he hoped the cop could help him out.

"No, no problem like that, but I can't find a location where I am supposed to make a delivery. Do you know where the Seward Greenhouse operation is located because I can't find it on my GPS? I normally don't do this route, but the regular guy called in sick, so they had me cover for him."

"You are in luck. You are only two turns and two miles away from the greenhouses. Just go straight until you hit your first light, there you turn right. At the next light, turn left, and you will see a large sign for Seward Greenhouse on your left side."

The driver thanked Danny and was on his way. Danny made his way back to the cruiser and made a note in his trip sheet. *At least I have something to put in, so I don't get accused of sleeping on the job. Score one more good deed for Danny Boy.*

Danny made a pass-through town and made a mental note that everything was still there. He thought about a similar night a lifetime ago that was just as quiet. The only difference was on that day there was snow on the ground, and the quiet was interrupted by a shotgun blast. Danny had been asking too many questions about the biggest case to ever hit Maidstone.

As Danny ran the details through his mind, he realized that he was once again looking for someone with a shotgun. Nothing was going on the night of the attack, just like tonight.

You are getting paranoid, buddy, Danny thought. But someone had tried to kill him back then, and tonight was just like that other night. Danny pulled over so he could make an entry about one of the traffic lights being out. As he was about to make his notation, he saw the previous entry about helping the truck driver.

Wait a minute. Why would a tank truck be going to Seward's Greenhouses? They had not been in operation since I got back from the Marines. It didn't sound illegal, just strange. Danny put the cruiser in gear and headed to the greenhouses. Just as he was about to make the last turn, he saw the tanker heading his way. The name on the side of the truck was McMillian Bulk Distributers, Westfield, MA.

Danny pulled in to the greenhouses, and they were just like he remembered them. None of them showed any sign of being used recently. Most of the plastic had long ago been ripped away by the wind and snow. Frames were crumpled from the winter weight. Weeds, trash and abandoned equipment filled out the rest of the landscape. There were three huge oil tanks near the office building. Danny exited the cruiser; and with his nightstick in hand, he went over to check the tanks. Each tank gave a dull thump in response to his banging. He expected a hollow echo, but to his surprise the tanks from the sound appeared to be full or at least have considerable fluid in them to dull the sound. Danny looked over the three huge tanks and tried to estimate just how much fuel they held. He was thinking just how much money was tied up in those three tanks. There had to be tens of thousands of dollars in fuel in the tanks at an abandon greenhouse complex, and there was no security.

Danny got out his FBI cell phone and began taking pictures. He knew he was on to something but had no idea what. All he knew was something was wrong. He took some measurements of the tanks and then got back in the cruiser. He left the greenhouses and headed back to the main part of town. Not too far from the greenhouses, Danny passed another tanker truck going the other way. This wasn't the big long-haul truck but a smaller home delivery type.

Where would this guy be going at this time of the night? It couldn't be an emergency delivery for someone who had run out as the night was fairly warm.

Danny watched the truck in his review mirror; and sure enough, the tanker made the turn toward the greenhouses. He made a quick U-turn and headed for a side road that passed to the rear of the greenhouses. Parking the cruiser, Danny made his way to a stone wall that bordered the complex. He took out a small set of Steiner binoculars and watched the oil tanks. At first, he thought that tanker was making a second delivery, but he soon realized the tanker was loading up, not dropping off. As the truck pulled away, he noted the name on the back, Prescott and Sons, Great Barrington, MA.

What the hell is going on here, Danny wondered. He made some notes for himself but not on his trip sheet. *Now what?*

Chapter 16

"We need to talk." It was Agent Deverse on the line but with no introduction.

"You call it. You know I am on midnights, so my days are wide open."

"How about we meet at the Butternut ski area? It's off season, and there will only be a few people around working on the grounds. Off to the left of the main lodge is an observation deck with some picnic tables. Bring Bear."

"Sounds good to me. Why bring Bear?"

"Of the two of you, I like Bear better. Plus, if anyone sees us, it just looks like we are out getting some exercise with the dog. See you in an hour?"

"I'll be there." Deverse clicked off, but the tone of the conversation left Danny wondering.

An hour later Danny pulled into the parking lot of Butternut Basin Ski Area. There were a few cars in the lot, but none over near the picnic table. Danny got out with Bear, and they made their way to the lower part of the slope to the picnic table sheltered by tall pines. Still no Deverse. Danny threw the ball for Bear a few times in different directions, checking things out looking to see if anyone was paying attention to them. The few people who were there seemed to be going about their business and not even glancing in Danny's direction. A short time later a pickup truck pulled in and parked near the base lodge. Out stepped Agent Deverse in blue jeans and sweat shirt. A camera hung from his neck. Agent Deverse made his way to the picnic table and joined Danny and Bear. The deck offered a full view of the parking area and the only way in. The tall pines made enough of a screen for anyone on the deck to buy them some time to disappear into the trees.

"No one followed you," announced Deverse.

"How do you know that--you were ten minutes behind me?"

"I picked you up at the three-way intersection and watched to see if anyone behind you made the turn. No one made that same turn for several cars so they wouldn't have seen you turn. Unless they put a GPS on the Jeep, they could not have followed you. Just in case they did, I went past the entrance and sat in the turn off and watched to see if anyone pulled up in that area and got out. That was also negative."

"So why are we meeting?"

"I hope you have some time. We got some things to go over. The names you turned up in your computer search were sent out to Fort Huachuca for a link analysis. You ever heard of a link analysis?"

"Yes, they talked about it down at Quantico, but as they went along, I realized that a department the size of Maidstone would not have enough information in their database to do a true link search. It would be used in a mob- type investigation or maybe espionage case. You sent this out to a spy agency?"

"They do investigations and active spying, but they are also a training center. Investigations are used as training scenarios for their students. They are searching real life people with actual addresses and associations. The FBI has its own link analyses team, but they are fully engaged in cases like you pointed out searching out the mob or terrorists. Your information gave them a starting place and a general direction. The information that comes from that will dictate the path to be followed.

"That analysis didn't show anything criminal. When you see the connections, you can draw the conclusion that there are number of people in a very general area who can influence things. There is a potential for information to be compromised. Back before the hit, one of Marvin Cohen's secretaries passed on information to one of the Worthington family members that the Penny Worthington murder was being re-examined. She fed the information back to Snyder and then things snowballed. She is a cousin in the Worthington family, but no one knew it. Two generations separate her from being a direct relation to the Worthington's and, of course, a different last name."

"So now what should we do?"

"What you do is review the analysis and see what connections you can come up with. The brains at Fort Huachuca have linked the people, but now it takes someone local to decide what those connections mean, if anything. Here's a flash drive with all the information. It's encrypted and password protected, so no one will be able to hack in, but don't lose it. Don't use the department's computers or your own. Head on down to Litchfield or somewhere else out of town to go over it. When you find something or when you decide there's nothing there, give me a call; and we will get together again."

Danny nodded his head and wondered if it was all worth it.

"You stay here for a half hour and play with Bear or walk around. I am going to head out and then double back and take up a post to see if anyone is watching you."

"Do you think this is all necessary?"

94

"Did someone try and cut you in half with a shotgun? Do you think the chief is out to get you? Do you think that something criminal is going on in this town? "

"Sorry I asked."

Agent Deverse departed, and Danny waited the half hour with his mind a tad clouded at this point.

Chapter 17

Danny made his way down to Litchfield in a roundabout way by first going into New York State. Pulling off Route 202, Danny parked at the main building for the White Memorial Foundation. There he waited for a few minutes to see if anyone pulled in behind him. It was midweek and early in the morning. The park was deserted except for a few caretakers who maintain the grounds and picked up trash. No one followed him in. Just in case, Danny exited the foundation property by a second driveway and headed for the library. The same cute librarian was there and gave him a warm smile. *She remembered*, thought Danny.

"More research?" she asked.

"Yes, but on some other things for school."

He had no idea what he was about to look at. His exposure to link analysis was down at the academy and covered more about understanding the results as opposed to creating the information. Danny settled in on the computer and loaded the flash drive. He was shocked when the information came up on the screen. Now this wasn't a small laptop screen, but an oversized desktop unit. The screen was even bigger than most full-size terminals. Even with the large screen there was so much information being presented that nothing was legible. He could make out what looked like names followed by several lines of information in a little block. All the blocks were interconnected by lines leading to a central block also with a name and information. Unfortunately, so much information was trying to fit on the page that none of it came up large enough to read.

The librarian saw the confused look on Danny's face and made her way over. Danny saw her approach out of the corner of his eye and was about to shut the page down when he realized that she wouldn't be able to see the words any better than he could. If he did shut it down, then the librarian might get suspicious and think he was doing something wrong like looking at porn. The librarian came up next to Danny just a bit closer than was necessary and asked, "Having trouble?"

Danny could feel her hand on his shoulder; and as she leaned in, her breast pressed against him.

"What in the world is that supposed to be?" She looked at the screen trying to read the tiny words, but even she couldn't understand what was on the screen.

"It is some sort of chart that they assigned me to work on at school. I don't think I am going to get too far with this."

"Try clicking on one of the blocks and see what happens."

Danny clicked on a box and sure enough the block with the name expanded and filled up the screen. There was the name clearly legible with a brief description as to who the person was. Danny was now concerned because the librarian might recognize the person and start asking questions. The name meant nothing to Danny, and then he saw the dates below the name: born 1/22/1912, died 4/14/1989.

"That looks like a dead end. Oh, that was a horrible pun."

Danny gave a small laugh, but he had to agree with her. Danny was trying to figure out how to make the librarian move away so he could get back to his research when an older female went up to the front desk and hit the bell for service.

"Duty calls. Let me know if you need any more help." With a warm smile and a slight back rub, she departed.

Danny moved the cursor around clicking on boxes and making notes. After a few dozen clicks, he realized that while there was a ton of information without seeing the links, this was going nowhere. Without the links, he could not see the relationship of one to the other or how that block related to the group. Danny closed out that screen and opened another folder. This one brought up the names in alphabetical order but without regard to dates. One person might still be alive according to the dates, and next person could be dead for 100 years. Danny scrolled through every name and nearly got motion sickness as he watched the passing lines disappear with the roll of the mouse. Then names started to mean something, names from the present. Danny made a word document and began copying and pasting the information. It didn't show a relationship, but the names stood out. In the end Danny had about 40 names on his list. He saved them to the flash drive and deleted the document. The information was probably still there somewhere on the computer, but it was never saved to a named location on the hard drive so it would take a real computer whiz to find it. Danny double checked everything to make sure he hadn't forgotten something and made for the door.

"I hope I see you again," was the departing call from the librarian.

Danny waved and smiled back. If I do come back, thought Danny, I better not have Geri with me. With that he was out the door.

Chapter 18

"What did you find?" asked Deverse when Danny called.

Where to start, thought Danny. "There is a ton of information in there, and I can't read the important stuff. The chart has so many people with cross connections that to get it on one computer screen is impossible. You can click on a person and that expands things, but you don't see the links. I have tried to follow them, but there is just too much info there."

"So, what do you want to do?"

"If they can, trim things down a bit. First, eliminate anyone born before 1920. We are looking for living connections. Second, track a list of people I know are related to see what gets added to the list. I have gone through the names made up in alphabetical order. I then went and highlighted known names. Because the list is alphabetical, there is no order to the list. I have no idea what the connection is."

"Okay, make your request and put the drive in your mailbox down in Great Barrington with your own address, so that the post office people don't try and take it in. I will pick it up and forward it on to the research people. As soon as I get a response, I will get back to you."

"Anything else?"

"Not right now." But there was more, a lot more. Taking a tip from the FBI, Danny decided that if they could hold out on him then there was no reason for him not to hold back. Dealing with the FBI is always a one-way street when it came to sharing information. That fact had almost gotten Danny killed. Besides, what Danny was finding out was not related to the FBI investigation. Now Danny was working directly for the FBI on a case of unknown size. He wanted to catch everyone who had been part of the murder-cover up, but now something else was going on. He was getting paid by the town, but he was putting in almost as much time working for the FBI for nothing. Danny wanted to do the right thing for the right reasons. He also knew that the FBI had more than enough money to cover his hours. They had made him a Special U. S. Marshall, so he would have federal protection. They had neglected to pay him for his services. If things turned out that there were more connections and Danny uncovered them, there would be more arrests. That would mean the end of Danny as a police officer. He was taking heat for being the good guy who almost got killed. More arrests would put him farther on the outside of the town.

Some of the names on the alphabetical list had stood out, and he had expected them to be there. The family names on the fuel trucks he spotted at the greenhouses were new, and he needed to find the connection.

Why would anyone be filling up fuel tanks at an abandoned greenhouse complex? Were they planning to restart the business? Who had the kind of money to invest in fuel and let it sit?

From the short time he had worked in a hardware store, Danny knew you had to turn products over, or you were wasting money with items sitting on a shelf. Granted you had to have an inventory on hand; but if you sold 100 gallons of paint a month, you didn't keep 500 gallons on hand just in case. Idle products cost you money when they didn't move.

Danny decided he needed to do some more checking on the greenhouses and those fuel tanks. After getting off shift Danny changed clothes, picked up Bear with the Jeep, and headed toward the greenhouses. The Seward Greenhouse complex was located in a farming area. There were also hiking trails in a marsh that had been donated to the town. With Bear as his cover story, no one would look twice at a guy walking his dog. Still Danny was on alert for anyone paying too much attention to him. It was easy enough to slip into the complex as the fence was in disrepair from kids breaking in to party or from the Berkshire winters that brought as much ice as it did snow. If there were a plan to restart the business, nothing had been done. There was no new construction or projects in sight. Danny made his way to the fuel tanks. There was some spillage down the side of the tank opening, and it was clearly diesel. Danny looked around and found the placard for the tank, which stated that it could hold up to ten thousand gallons. Danny took a quick picture of it with his FBI cellphone. At this point Danny had all the information he had come for and made his exit the way he came in. He did not want to stay any longer than was necessary just in case. At the fence line there was a slight rise, and Danny used the elevation to take a few seconds of video just to document the disrepair and the size of the tanks.

"Okay, buddy," Danny said to Bear, "let's get outta here."

Bear didn't mind leaving the complex, but he wasn't ready to get back in the Jeep. After being alone all night in the barn, he was ready to do some exploring and some ball chasing. So, Danny got out the tennis ball and began a game of fetch. Bear could chase the ball for hours. Unfortunately, Danny needed to get back to the barn and get some sleep after a long night and an extended morning. Bear came back with the last fetch, and Danny told him to load up. Bear hung back hoping for one last throw, but Danny insisted. Reluctantly Bear got into the Jeep. Danny had one foot in the Jeep when he heard a vehicle approaching down in the area of the greenhouses. Danny picked up the binoculars and scanned the truck as it pulled up to the fuel tanks. This was a smaller home delivery truck with the name Superior Fuels, Pittsfield, MA.

What is going on here, Danny wondered? To Bear's delight, the ball came back out; and the game was on once again. But Danny was concentrating on the truck and not Bear's excitement. The fuel truck was there for close to one half hour. Based on where the truck had made the connection, it was taking fuel on not dropping it off. Danny made some quick notes and snapped a few photos. Then it was back to the barn and some much-needed sleep. Thinking about the events kept him awake much of the morning.

Chapter 19

Danny gave Agent Deverse a call to see what progress the spooks at Fort Huachuca had made. He was also going to bring up the subject of getting paid. He felt guilty about asking; but on the flip side, he was putting in a lot of time for the FBI and getting nothing in return except for investigative help. If this mess blew up, he would be out of a job in a heartbeat. Depending on how bad he got trashed, he might not be able to stay in Maidstone. Everyday there was a chance that Danny would do something that might get him fired or suspended. The chief could always see a violation as being insubordination and recommend firing. One cross word to a motorist or one messed up report could be Monday morning quarterbacked to death. The chief had already tried to catch Danny sleeping on the job. Danny always had a micro recorder in his pocket, just in case. Anytime he was in contact with the public, he would switch it on for a little added protection. He hated living that way, but it was the smart thing to do.

"Well," asked Danny, "what do you have for me?"

"The people out at Huachuca set it up a few ways. They are working with a big screen computer like six feet by four feet. For them it was easy to see all the connections on a screen that size. They also have a printer that can print that big, and they sent me a copy. They broke it down as you asked and that does show up on a normal computer screen. They took it a few steps further and made sub-charts with identified hubs."

"What is an identified hub?"

"When the data points back to a hub, or in this case a central figure, they isolate that hub and that person's direct connections. It makes viewing the charts less confusing. If they are listed on one of the charts, they have a connection with Covington Worthington at some point. It is hard to explain over the phone, but once you see that charts, it is like a light going on. I will set a meeting place where we can view them."

"Anything new on your end with the chief or anyone else?"

"Nothing stands out. The chief has been keeping his distance. I don't think anyone is after me in a direct way right now. I am not seeing the same cars or people showing up all the time. No one is asking me strange questions. The calls I am being sent on are just your typical midnight shift calls. The chief seems to be preoccupied with the new house he can't afford. He is trying to dump his condo. But I did run across some unusual activity on the midnight shift.

"How so?"

"It was late at night, and there was this tanker truck idling in the middle of town. I knew if he stayed there too long, we would be getting a call about the noise and diesel smell, so I checked to see if he was lost. Come to find out, he was looking for an address for Seward's Greenhouses. It wasn't in his GPS. That was easy enough, and I gave him directions to the place."

"And how is that unusual?"

"The greenhouses haven't been used in over three years. I went down and sure enough the tanker pulled in and was unloading. There are three ten-thousand-gallon fuel tanks on the property. That place used to be a huge operation back in the day; but when the old man died, the kids didn't want any part of it."

"Is someone planning on restarting the operation?"

"It doesn't appear that way. Everything is a mess. It is overgrown with weeds and abandoned equipment. The plastic roofs are all shredded and flapping in the wind. No one has done anything to the office. The only sign of activity is around the three fuel tanks. It is the only place where the weeds are beaten down. Now here is the kicker. The guy I gave directions to was in a full-size tractor trailer tanker--a bulk delivery type that you would see filling up a gas station. After this guy leaves, a smaller tank truck pulls in--the size you would see making home deliveries."

"Dropping off more fuel?"

"No, this guy looked like he was filling up. If you have a pen, I will give you the names on the trucks. There were actually two small trucks that pulled in and loaded up. None of the names on the trucks were the same."

"Who owns the greenhouse?"

"It was the Seward family, but it might have changed hands at some point when the kids decided not to take over the business. The records would be in town hall, but I don't want to go in there and raise suspicion. I'd say the greenhouses haven't been used in at least three years since I have been back here, but it could be a lot longer than three years because that is when I got home. It could have been any time up to six years before that when I left for the Marines."

"Go on the computer and check Vision Appraisals," said Deverse. "A lot of small towns like Maidstone farm out their tax assessments and property appraisals to that company. Maidstone might be one. There isn't a footprint left if you access their website so no one will get a notification that you had checked that way. Whatever you do, don't do it on a computer where someone could check your browser history. I will run the names on the trucks."

"You will make connections. I know at least on one of them has a family connection up here."

"I hate to bring this up, but I am putting in a lot of hours for the Feds."

"I was just getting to that. You are officially on the payroll from the day you got back to Maidstone. You need to keep track of your hours, expenses, and what you were doing related to this investigation. It doesn't matter if you are on duty at the time so long as you can relate activity to this case."

Danny was surprised and relieved. He hadn't planned on the FBI taking care of him. He didn't want to sound like a mercenary working this case for money. He still didn't feel completely right about this, but it was their idea without Danny having to make demands or even a suggestion.

"Check out Vision and get back to me."

Before Danny could ask one more question, the line went dead. *How much am I going to get paid,* he wondered? *Well, it's more than what I thought I was making before which was zero so I guess I will just have to wait and see. I am not going to spend a penny of that money. It is all going into a bank somewhere, just in case.*

Now Danny had to find a computer. Litchfield was a bit of a haul and while it might be nice to see the touchy, friendly librarian again, she might read a little too much into it. Or maybe she would read it just right. How did things ever get this complicated?

Chapter 20

Danny made his way down to the Scoville Library in Salisbury, Connecticut. It was just as nice as Litchfield and without the interesting librarian with the nerdy glasses. Danny though he would need help searching through Vision Appraisals, but it was quite simple and strait forward so even he could figure it out.

He found an old newspaper article about the closing of the Seward Greenhouses shortly after he enlisted in the Marines. The article lamented that the family business of over 100 years was closing for good. But there was nothing, not even a short story, about the sale. Danny accessed Vision Appraisal, and there was the real estate card. Unfortunately, it didn't give him the answers he was looking for. No individual names came up. Danny copied the information to his flash drive and printed out a copy. The new owner was listed as Berkshire Hills Quick Green. The transaction was listed as of four years ago. It was an LLC, and all the listed officers were attorneys' offices with the CFO being an accounting firm. On the upside, they were all local.

There was a whole lot of information that told nothing. The place went under almost nine years ago. It was sold, but no one had done anything with the place. That meant there was a lot of property on which to pay taxes and maybe insurance but not use. Four years ago, some of the buildings and greenhouses were productive but not now. It might be cheaper to tear the place down and start all over.

Danny stopped in to see his old boss at the hardware store. Old man Elwood was glad to see him. It was always nice to know someone on the force. Danny's career in hardware hadn't lasted very long. He was not the handyman type and for the most part couldn't help the customers. In some cases, he didn't even know if they were talking electrical or plumbing.

"So, how's business going?" asked Danny.

"Not getting rich but the bills are getting paid, and there is always some money left over at the end of the month. I just pray that they don't let Lowes come into town. Now that would kill me."

Danny had a flash. "Are they talking about the Seward Greenhouses for a location?"

"Not that I know of, but damn, that would be the spot I would pick now that you mention it."

Danny filed that tidbit away for future reference. Maybe that was what going on but why thirty thousand gallons for diesel? "How is the fuel oil business going?" asked Danny.

"Oh, I have to stay on top of that almost every day. The prices change, the demand goes up or down, and my competitors keep coming up with savings plans. Don't get me wrong, I do make money; but I have to monitor what is going on. If I had bigger tanks, I could get bigger bulk deliveries. The more they sell in one load, the better the price for me."

"Between the home heating oil deliveries and filling up customer's trucks, has that meant some serious bucks coming in?"

"You're not comparing apples with oranges, but you are mixing apples. That isn't permitted," said Elwood. "They are both the same fuel, but home heating oil has a dye in it to identify it from diesel truck fuel. Truck fuel has state and federal taxes added to the cost on top of the sales tax. Home heating oil doesn't."

"How much of a difference?"

"That depends," said Elwood. "It can vary between sixty cents to almost a dollar. The more you buy, the less they charge you for a gallon. The state and federal taxes go up and down at times. If I were a gutsy individual and I knew I wouldn't get caught, I would be selling home heating oil to truckers. I could sell it cheaper so I could get lots of customers looking to save money. Down side is it would only take one person to rat me out. Then the state and federal authorities would be all over me. I don't need to see the IRS any more than I already do."

"Could you really make big bucks doing that?"

"Those big rigs only get six miles to the gallon. You do the math. For every six miles, you might be saving thirty to forty cents. When you're doing long haul trucking, you are racking up some serious miles. If you have construction equipment, you might not be getting lots of miles, but the equipment will be running all day using fuel. It is a great scam so long as you don't get caught."

"I guess. Having never been a home owner or a truck driver, I wouldn't have thought of that."

Unfortunately, there is always a *but*. The big truck was dropping off and smaller home delivery trucks were picking up. It should have been the other way around if they were running this scam, thought Danny.

Chapter 21

"Danny, your other phone is going to ring. Don't answer it," shouted Deverse over the FBI phone.

Sure enough, as he spoke the last words the phone began to ring. Danny looked down and saw that it was the chief's direct line. Oh shit, this can't be good, Danny thought; and he silenced the ring.

"Okay, Deverse, what the hell is this all about?"

"Did you spend some time on and off duty checking out some abandoned greenhouses?"

Danny's mind was on overdrive. How could Deverse know, and why would the chief be calling? But Danny thought a few seconds too long, and Deverse had no patience at this point.

"Would you please say *yes* or fucking *no*? This shit is important."

In all the time Danny had been associated with Agent Deverse, he had never raised his voice or used a swear word. "Yes, I did check out the greenhouses. There is something strange going on there. It......." But Deverse cut him off.

"We will talk details later, but right now you need to know they have you on video. When the chief asks you if you were there, don't fucking lie. Tell him something that will cover why you were there and why you went back off duty.

They know you took pictures, and they may ask to see your phone. You used the FBI phone for photos, I hope?"

"Yes, it was the FBI phone." Danny was no longer confused, but knew he had to think fast. "You said they have me on video. Who would *they* be?"

"I have a hunch, but that doesn't matter right now. All you need to know is someone has an interest in the greenhouses, and the chief is going to be pumping you for information. This guy called the chief and was very concerned, specifically about you being there and taking pictures. Now hang up and call the chief. Don't lie, but if you found something don't give it up. Don't give him anything that will make him think you are holding back. Got it?"

"Not really but, oh shit."

"Yeah really, oh shit. You can't wait too long before you call him back; he is getting antsy."

"How the hell do you know he is getting antsy?"

"Call, I'll explain later," and the line went dead.

Danny quickly dialed the chief's number. "Sorry, chief, I was making a head call. What can I do for you?"

"I need you to come into the station," said the chief.

"Roger that. Is everything okay?"

"We will talk when you get here," and again the line went dead.

Danny looked at the phone and tried to translate the chief's voice and what he really meant--short, abrupt with some aggravation mixed in. Then there was Agent Deverse. He knew things before they happened. He already knew where Danny had been and what he was up to. But, so did someone else, and Danny guessed that person wasn't with the FBI. Danny tried to drive slowly back to the station running through his mind what he would tell the chief. Danny reviewed his activity and what his actions would have looked like if he were on video. He didn't have any pictures of the greenhouse area on his civilian phone. That could be easily explained as he decided to delete them because he didn't need them. He took the close ups of the plaques on the tanks, so he could see the type and size that they were. That was true enough, but he could explain he deleted them when he realized they were of no value. But going back after work, why? Daylight, I wanted to see things in the light of day. Something I might have missed in the dark. But there was nothing new to see, so Danny would tell the chief he dropped it and went home.

It wasn't much of a plan, but Danny was back at the station and out of time. *I must have really stepped in something if in just a few days everything had gotten back to the chief.*

Danny knocked on the chief's door. "Come," was the bark from inside.

The chief didn't offer Danny a seat and got right to it. "What were you doing out at the old greenhouses the other night? I got a report of suspicious activity that a police officer was snooping around out there."

Danny tried to play it cool as if no big deal. "Chief, I found a truck driver who was lost, and he asked directions to Seward's Greenhouses. I told him the directions; and after he left, it dawned on me that the place had been closed for years so I went out there to see if he had the right greenhouses. I guess it was the right place because he saw me as he was leaving the complex and didn't ask for more help."

"So, what did you do?"

"Seeing that I was out there I figured I would have a look around. The place is long past being trashed. Between the kids over the years looking for a place to party and the weather, the complex was a mess."

"The person reporting the suspicious activity said a guy and a dog were there during the day, was that you?" the chief wanted to know.

"Yep, that was probably me. I had to take Bear out for a walk, and I was still trying to figure out what he guy was doing there. I thought that in the dark I might have missed something but when I looked things over in the daylight, it all seemed okay. The place was still a mess, but I couldn't find anything new that might have just happened."

"You take any pictures?" the chief asked.

"Yeah, I took some shots of the tanks. I couldn't read the plaques at the angle I was on, so I used the cellphone to see around the corner. Nothing earth shattering there. Just numbers and manufactures information."

"Where are the pictures now?"

"I deleted them. They were of no use, so I dumped them."

The chief wanted to check the phone, but couldn't come up with a reason to ask. To his surprise, Danny pulled out his phone, opened it to the photo app, and handed it to the chief. The surprised chief took the phone and after a quick glance noted that the most recent pictures were several weeks old. With a grunt, he gave the phone back to Danny.

The chief eyed Danny for a long moment. He had a lot more questions, but couldn't ask them without raising concern. Danny for his part tried to look as innocent as possible and be seen as fully cooperative with nothing to hide.

"Okay. That is all. Next time you are doing a patrol check, leave your running lights on and call it in. I didn't see an entry in the log for the directions for the trucker or that you were out there checking the area. If something happened to you, we would not have known where to go looking for you."

"Yes, sir," was Danny's military response, and he was out the door.

113

Chapter 22

Danny was heading for his Jeep as fast as he could without looking like he was in a hurry. If anyone saw him, no one would think twice about his getting out of the building. No one liked to be called in the chief's office, and the tension between Danny and the chief was no secret. Still Danny wanted answers. How could Deverse know that the chief would be calling? How did he know where he had been snooping around the greenhouses? Then the FBI phone rang.

Even before Danny could say hello, Agent Deverse cut him off. "I know you have a million plus questions, but not right now and not in a few minutes when you get away from the station. You did a great job in there. It sounds like they bought it, and nothing more will come of it for now. I will meet you down at the Hopkins Inn at Lake Waramaugh. I will see you down there at seven. Go into the bar and wait. I will be along shortly after."

Danny was stammering trying to frame a question, but there were too many.

"Fine," and Danny hit the off button. Danny looked around, but didn't see anything unusual or anyone out of place. He looked at his phone, one of the few things the FBI had given him. Was the phone really a bug, he wondered? *No, wait,* Danny thought. *Deverse knew all about the chief and the call coming from him. Holy shit, the whole friggin place is bugged!* Then he remembered Deverse's orders about using the phone and getting away from everything that was part of the police department. Danny thought Deverse was warning him that the PD might try to bug him. Maybe they might, but now for sure it was the FBI. Danny was pissed. First the FBI doesn't tell him that there is a mob hit on him that very nearly succeeds. Now he is being wiretapped by the people he is supposed to be working for. They obviously didn't trust him to the point they had him bugged to see what he was doing. And the FBI were the ones that wanted his help. Danny was the one sticking his neck out. He was now on a case about oil trucks doing who knows what. This was supposed to be an investigation about the payoff to Lieutenant Snyder. He wasn't getting anywhere near to the lieutenant's pay off to bag the murder case. The FBI didn't seem to care. Oh, shit, another thought popped into Danny's head. Where else had he been on video that has a connection to the chief? Why would the chief care that he was out at the old greenhouses? Apparently, someone does, and that person is close enough to the chief that in short order he is standing tall in front of the man explaining himself. Danny couldn't think of any connection between the chief and the greenhouses. The ownership records were a corporate dead end with just law offices and accounts listed as members of the corporation.

Danny got to the Hopkins Inn early and went into the winery. The young lady behind the counter was cute and wanted to know if Danny wanted to do a wine tasting. Danny really wanted to hit the bar across the street and have a double scotch, but the winery offered a better view of anyone approaching and checking out the parking lots.

"Why sure," said Danny. "Something not too dry and also not too sweet. Can you fix me up?"

"The tasting is for five different wines, but I would say that only three meet your requirements. How about if I pour the three; whichever one you like the best, I will just fill your glass. How does that sound?"

"You're not trying to get me drunk?" asked Danny.

"Maybe later," was the quick response followed by a slight grin.

The timing wasn't lost on Danny. He was up to his asshole in alligators with the FBI, had a great girlfriend, and getting hit on. *They must know somehow*, he thought. Maybe she is part of the bugging detail. He looked up, and there aimed right at him was a surveillance camera. He looked around the room and saw several more. With each discovery, he became that much more wired. If the clerk noticed, she didn't show it. Danny took a sip of wine that tasted very smooth. He could have used the bite of scotch, but that would be later. "Very nice," he said. The young lady smiled back and poured the next sample. Danny let the wine set in and thought that he should just stay right there--sipping wine and checking out the lovely young lady. Talking with Agent Deverse was not going to be as pleasant. Here he is, working for the FBI as a sworn officer, and he is under surveillance the whole time. Didn't they trust him? What did they think he was up to? The chief wants my head, and the FBI is tracking me like I am the target of this investigation. Wasn't he the one to get shot at?

Chapter 23

Danny was looking out the window of the winery where he saw Deverse pull into the inn. Danny watched as he got out of the vehicle and noticed that he checked out Danny's jeep in the parking lot across from the winery. Danny alternated between watching Deverse and checking out the road that went past the inn and the winery. Deverse disappeared into the Inn, but Danny still held his post inside the tasting room. After several minutes Deverse reappeared with a puzzled look on his face.

He must have checked in and scouted out the bathroom, thought Danny. Now he is wondering where the hell I am. Danny watched for a minute or two more as Agent Deverse scanned the parking area and the vineyard hills behind. Finally, Danny saw Agent Deverse reach for his cell and that was Danny's cue that he had waited long enough. Before Deverse could dial the cell phone, Danny stepped out of the tasting room and waved him over. Deverse pocketed the phone and walked over with a what-gives/annoyed look on his face. Deverse entered the tasting room and locked eyes with Danny. It was clear Deverse wasn't thrilled with his simple instructions not being followed and then made to wait and wonder where Danny was.

"I am watching who might be watching," Danny said in a low voice.

"Why?" Deverse wanted to know. He was not pleased, and for the first time, things seemed tense between the two.

"I am being wire tapped and monitored by the people I am supposed to be working with," said Danny. "I thought I was part of the team, and that you were here to support me-- not spy on me. Now I am looking over my shoulder more than ever wondering whose side I am on or if I am out here being used by both sides. This was supposed to be an investigation into who paid off Lieutenant Snyder, but now it looks like I am the one being investigated. So, what is going on?"

Agent Deverse was about to answer when he noticed the young lady paying attention to the conversation. "Let's take this up in the bar," and he gave a slight nod in the young lady's direction.

Danny wanted answers but also more control. "How about we just step outside and see how it goes from there. I just might be done with this whole thing right now."

Agent Deverse thought of his options and what had happened in the past few days. Yes, Danny might think he was being played, and he had to do some quick talking to make things right.

"Two minutes in the parking lot, and then we go in for dinner," said Deverse. "If I can't convince you in two minutes, then an hour won't help."

"Two minutes, it's all yours," and they exited the tasting room.

As they departed the winery, the young lady followed them out the door with her eyes. They crossed the road and stood in the parking lot away from the vehicles. Danny was not about to get in or near any vehicle.

"So?" was Danny's only question.

119

"Remember when you first got back here, and I gave you the cell phone and some instructions?"

Danny though back. "Yeah, you told me not to use it in the PD, the cruiser, and away from the portable radio."

Agent Deverse looked at Danny and raised his eyebrows, then gave him a shoulder shrug. "Why do you think I said that?"

Danny just stared at Agent Deverse and gave no response. Deverse would be answering the questions, not Danny.

Not getting an answer, Deverse went on. "Remember walking into the PD that first day and seeing that brand new control center with new radios and new computers?"

The image popped into Danny's brain of all the new equipment that had been installed in less than three months-- equipment that had not been ordered or even discussed. In less than three months, it was up and running at no expense to the town. There were thousands of dollars of equipment that the department was to test and evaluate for free. Slowly, what was going on began to sink in. "No way."

"Absolutely," replied Deverse. "It is all FBI equipment, and we can monitor everything going on in the department except the bathrooms. When I called to warn you about the chief calling, it was the chief being monitored, not you. When I knew you had pulled it off with the chief's interview, it was his computer that was feeding us the information, not you being wired. As soon as you left, even before you were out the front door, the chief was on the phone to Quenton briefing him on everything that was said in the room. You did a very convincing job, and for the most part they buy it. One thing you can't do is go back to the greenhouses or follow tanker trucks."

"You bugged the entire police department?" Danny asked in disbelief.

"We already had most of the equipment from a gambling/narcotics investigation. It was a simple matter to make the offer to the police department with no strings attached. The fact that we required detailed reports on use and activity almost killed the deal. While the reporting almost got the chief to back out, it added to the credibility that it was a real deal. When the town fathers heard that they were getting thousands of dollars' worth of free equipment, they jumped on it and insisted that Cornell take the deal. There was no way he was going to say no to them. They didn't care if the cops had to write up some extra reports as long as they got this gear for free and could stand up at the town meeting and take credit for such a fantastic deal. Now can we go in and get a scotch and some wiener schnitzel? The company is picking up the tab so don't get the bar scotch." Agent Deverse put his arm around Danny and directed him to the door of the Inn.

For his part Danny was speechless. He kept forming questions, but in the end all that came out was, "You bugged an entire police department?"

"Trust me, it was easy."

Chapter 24

"You have been listening in on everything the police department has been doing for months?" Danny wanted to know, still in total disbelief.

"The short answer is *yes,* for the most part. To be completely fair, we cut back on a lot of phone lines and the radio. There are persons of interest, shall I say, who we are on 24/7. The chief is the main person, and we listen in on his computer, desk phone, cell phone, and his vehicle radio. In all the airtime at the beginning, we were getting just routine, everyday normal stuff. Some of it was very interesting as in very juicy gossip, but it wasn't of a criminal nature."

Danny took a sip of his twelve-year-old scotch and gave it a very slow swallow. "How in the world did you get a judge to sign-off on a wiretap for an entire police department?"

"After the mob tried to take you out on Lieutenant Snyder's request, it was fairly easy to convince a judge that more people in the police department had to be involved. No one thought Snyder could pull something off like this all by himself. In truth, he did have a lot of help. He didn't pull it off all by himself, but the people who were helping him were not doing it for criminal reasons. Some thought they were just doing the good lieutenant a favor--a favor that they were almost always rewarded for. People just thought of the lieutenant as a very generous guy. No one up in Maidstone knew about the mob safe-house meetings. They just had it in their minds that some big shot executives were coming to town and didn't want to be disturbed. They never met any of Snyder's guests. These houses would be set aside, fully stocked with whatever Snyder ordered; and when empty, the place was cleaned and ready to use again. These guys were mobsters, not rock stars. No one was tearing the place up or throwing TVs out the window if they didn't like the show. Heck, they even smoked their cigars out under the pergolas so there wasn't any hint of smoke inside. They were very considerate for organized crime bosses. When the judge saw all the information we had, he didn't even finish reading it before he signed the warrant. Then we listened around the clock for weeks, but nothing was coming out connecting anyone to the hit or the mob boss meetings. The guys on the department should be a little more careful about what they say on the department phones and in the building."

"How's that?"

"You know, the talk about wives, girlfriends, other officers. It got very descriptive at times."

Oh shit, thought Danny. *What had he said over the last few months?* "If you haven't made a connection in this amount of time, how is it that they let you keep listening? Most wire taps have an expiration date, or you have to show just cause why the wire is still needed."

"Right you are. That is where we made the connection between the Chief and Quenton. Seems there are favors being done this time by Cornell for old man Worthington. This thing with the greenhouses has Quenton spooked, and he wants you and the PD kept away from the place. I don't think Cornell even knows why, but he is doing whatever Quenton asks because he really likes the idea of having that new house.

Let's move this into the dining room. There is a lot more background noise in there just in case someone hears us."

They finished their scotches and moved to the front of the inn with a window view of the lake. The scene outside was calm and peaceful. Danny was in a hurricane in his brain.

"When you checked out the greenhouses, was there anything besides the fuel tanks that looked like it might be being used?"

"No, the place was a mess. The weather and the kids sneaking in to party or see what they could steal have left the place totally trashed."

"What about the brick office building?"

"It's there. It is probably the only thing still standing, but it is sealed off. All the windows have been bricked over. The doors are super heavy duty, and they have those big padlocks with the metal hoods so you can't get bolt cutters on them."

"What about electricity? Are there any wires running to the building?"

Danny thought for a moment and then pulled out his FBI cell phone. He flipped through the apps until he got to the photos and began to scroll through them. At one photo he stopped and enlarged the screen. He handed the phone to Deverse. "It looks like there are wires running from the street to the brick building and then over to the fuel tanks. I can't be sure, but that is what it looks like."

Deverse reviewed the photos and the others on the phone. "Yes, it does look like there could be power out there. Quenton has something to do with the greenhouses, though at this point we don't know what. He did not like you poking around. First thing the next morning, he was in the coffee shop with Cornell, and the conversation was rather heated. It was also short with Cornell hustling off to his office. Now, that conversation we couldn't hear, but a short time later

Quenton was on the phone to Cornell wanting to know what you were doing there that night and why you came back in the morning in civilian clothes. That is when you got the call to report to the chief's office. For now, keep an eye on the tanker trucks but don't call them in and don't follow them. And watch your back. From the tone of his voice, Quenton is really pissed at you; and Cornell is doing whatever Quenton tells him. I don't think Cornell would do you physical harm, but he will do everything in his power to jam you up. Quenton Worthington sounded like he would strangle you with his bare hands. Owning a trucking company also puts him in touch with a lot of teamsters. Some of those union/management confrontations are just for show. Here they are management and the union trashing each other when the news cameras are rolling. The next thing you know they are sharing cocktails at the country club. So, watch yourself," said Deverse. "It doesn't have to be a hit or anything physical coming at you. Maybe it's a favor you do that crosses the line. Or you get baited into saying something unprofessional that could get you suspended or fired. Someone on or off duty starts messing with you, and when they hit the right button, the cell phone camera comes on to document the whole thing. If it is between Cornell and Worthington, it's a good bet we will have their plan recorded. But if they farm it out, then you are on your own."

Danny took it all in. This was far more than he ever expected in Maidstone. Even after getting shot at, this new twist did not seem real. Had all this been going on when he was growing up here, he asked himself. It must have been; he just never saw it and wasn't part of it.

Chapter 25

Danny stayed out of sight on the midnight shift. Most mornings he would be done and out of the station an hour before the chief arrived. He kept up his activity, but refrained from pulling anyone over in a remote area. He called in his patrol checks and made notes in his trip sheet. If anyone were checking on him, he would look like any other officer. On occasion he would have to hold over for the day shift where his path might cross with Chief Cornell. Danny did his best to stay under the radar.

On a Thursday night there was a stag for one of the officers getting married. It was held in the back room of the Butternut Brewery. The typical sausage and pepper tray was laid out with the ziti and kegged beer. Everything was going fine until a tray of shots came out. A second tray of Jägermeister came out, and Danny knew it was time to exit stage left. The beer sucked, and Danny had been holding the same glass the entire night. The shots now were something else, and he had to down it with everyone else or he would hear about it. When Danny saw the second round coming, he made a fast exit for the men's room. He could hear the chanting from inside and waited for the quiet when everyone would be chugging it down. He added another minute to his stay in the men's room then made his exit. His intent was to hit the door and keep going; but as he exited, he accidently bumped into a young lady. The bump resulted in a full martini being dumped all over the front of her, and she was pissed. Some of the gin made it onto Danny's back.

"Watch where you are going, asshole," were the first words spoken by the now wet and irate young lady.

"I am so sorry, I didn't see you," was all Danny could think to say.

She began to wipe up the mess with a napkin. Danny couldn't help but notice that the blouse was low cut and that she was wearing a black bra with a white shirt. It was something that would have stood out even without the gin soaking through.

"Well, the least you can do is replace my drink," she said.

"Yes, of course," said Danny as they moved up to the bar. He looked around quickly, and no one was paying them any attention. The accident had gone unnoticed. It appeared that the young lady was there alone. He didn't recognize her as a local. They got to the bar, and Danny ordered her drink.

"Aren't you going to have one?" Standing at the bar but facing Danny, any movement resulted in contact—contact that appeared to be on purpose.

"No, I am fine for now." But she insisted, and a scotch was ordered. Danny took a careful sip with no intention of drinking it down. The young lady never took her eyes off of Danny, and eventually Danny had to look back. She was put together very nicely, though a little extra heavy on the makeup. The two managed small talk, and in very short order, she finished her martini. Danny found out that her name was Tina and that she was up here alone for a short vacation. Tina had a slight New York City accent that she tried to hide. She was a tad older than she was trying to look.

"Buy me one more, and I will forget all about slamming into me."

Danny was about to protest the slamming part of the contact. In the first place, she was to the side and behind Danny and had walked into him. The hair on Danny's neck was going up at about the time Tina stepped closer to him making contact and then turning back towards the bar with her breast gently sliding across his arm.

"Sure thing, I will be right back. I have to check out with the guys in the backroom. It will only take a second."

"Hurry back, I don't want one of these guys hitting on me."

Danny gave as big a smile as he could. He put the scotch down and was about to head out the back door when he thought better of it. Danny raised his glass in salute. He put the glass to his lips but did not take a sip. Before Tina could say anything else, he was through the door and into the backroom. Things were still in high gear, and one of the guys offered him a shot. Danny raised his glass of scotch and declined the offer. In a heartbeat he kept moving and was out the backdoor and tucked into the shadows. He was about to toss the scotch, but thought better of it. He found a cinder block that was used to anchor the overhead canopy and slipped the scotch inside the opening. He found a flier stapled to the wall and used it to hide the glass. Danny scanned the parking lot but did not see anyone or hear any vehicles running.

Keeping to the shadows, Danny made his way to one of the closed craft shops on the far side of the parking lot. He found a picnic table under an overhang that was partially shielded by some latticework. Danny parked himself on the back side of the bench. He was in total darkness. Anyone looking across the parking lot directly at him would see nothing but a black void. If anyone walked toward him all he had to do was lay down on the bench, and he would be completely out of sight. Danny surveyed his Jeep and could not see anything unusual. He had parked the Jeep under a light and away from the other vehicles. It was a habit he had gotten into and parked that way routinely. He sat there patiently waiting to see what would happen next. It didn't take more than a minute or two before Tina exited the main entrance into the parking lot. She was not happy and was yelling into her cellphone.

"How the fuck should I know where he is," Tina's voice boomed across the parking lot. "I had him going in the bar. He said he had to check with the guys in the back room, and he never came out. I stuck my head in there, but he was gone. I even checked out the men's room. He wasn't there, but I did get a few offers. His Jeep is still here, but he is long gone."

Tina kept at it. "Fuck you, asshole. I've been picking up guys since I was fourteen. I know what the fuck I'm doing. Maybe this guy is gay. All I know is I had him pinned, and he got away. No, I don't know where. Fuck you. I want my money."

Danny gave himself a slight chuckle at that statement. Then things took a bad turn. Tina lit a cigarette while talking on the phone. The problem was she was walking strait towards Danny's hiding place. *Shit*, thought Danny. *Maybe she is going to come over here and sit down and wait to be picked up.* Danny moved flat on the bench and then slowly edged under the table. He heard the unmistakable sound of a key fob being used to unlock a car door. At the beep, a Cadillac's lights came on and doors unlocked. The vehicle was just off to the side of Danny's hiding position, and now he was lit up by the headlights. Fortunately for Danny, Tina was too busy yelling at her cell phone to notice him. She got in, started it up, and was gone throwing gravel in the air from her spinning tires. Once again, the lot went dark. Danny did manage to get the

New York license plate number. That explained the New York City accent that Tina tried to hide.

For the next hour Danny sat there watching as people left the bar. A Great Barrington cruiser pulled in and scanned the parking lot with its spotlight. *Nothing unusual with that, he thought. I do the same thing up in Maidstone every night.* Then Danny stopped breathing. The cruiser stopped at Danny's Jeep and played the spotlight over it. No other vehicle got that kind of special attention. It lasted only a few seconds, but it was more than enough to put Danny on edge. The cruiser departed and headed north out of the lot.

This is turning into a real buzzard fuck, though Danny. He watched a while longer then got out of his hiding spot and made for the Jeep.

I am glad this night is over, thought Danny as he exited the parking lot and headed back to Maidstone. But the night wasn't over.

Chapter 26

Danny wasn't more than a few thousand yards up the road when a police vehicle pulled out and lit him up. Danny knew beyond a shadow of doubt that this was a setup. First there was the babe in the bar followed by the cruiser checking out his Jeep. This cruiser had been stationed on the side of the road, and as soon as Danny had passed, it pulled out with all lights turned on. Danny slowed down and pulled over just off the road. He reached down and fingered his cell phone. *Shit, he thought. How many times do I press the button to get it to record?* The spotlight on the cruiser was aimed at the driver's side and was reflecting off the side mirror. The officer approached, but Danny could only see vague movement in the blinding light.

Then most of the light was blocked as the officer stepped up to the Jeep. "License, registration, and insurance card," the officer demanded.

"I am on the job," said Danny, "and I am armed."

"Where is the gun?" the voice in the darkness ordered.

"In my waistband in the small of my back."

"Don't touch it."

"No, sir, I won't. My police ID is in my left rear pocket, and my driver's license is in my right rear pocket. What would you like me to do?"

"Step out of the Jeep and keep your hands where I can see them."

Danny exited the vehicle in a very slow manner. This guy had to know who he was. There are only so many police officers in Great Barrington and Maidstone. At some point they had to have met. Danny faced the officer, and at that point he knew something was very wrong. The officer was wearing a white shirt. White shirts were all lieutenants and above. Lieutenants were not known to make routine traffic stops. Yes, they did stop vehicles from time to time, but it was usually for something serious. Any time a patrolman heard one of the brass making a traffic stop, the patrol officer would head that way. It had to be something worthwhile for a lieutenant to pull a vehicle over.

The officer shined the light in Danny's eyes temporarily blinding him. "Looks like you have been out partying tonight. How much have you had to drink?"

"One beer."

"That's strange," said the officer, "because I smell gin. You want to change your story or keep lying to me?"

Danny was about to protest, but it would be his word against the on-duty uniformed officer. Danny had just left a stag, and those parties always resulted in the excess consumption of beer. If you paid twenty bucks for a ticket, you wanted to get your money's worth. "I had a martini spilled on me," said Danny.

"Right," was the condescending reply. "I am going to administer a field sobriety breath test." The officer tucked his flashlight under his arm and reached into his pocket for the test unit. That's when Danny noticed this wasn't a lieutenant but a captain. Captains don't do drunk driving stops. When they spot a drunk, a patrolman is called for backup and to make the arrest. There is way too much paperwork for a

132

captain. He might make the stop, but then it would be up to the patrolman to do the dirty work.

"No field test before you want my breath?"

"Don't be a smart ass, or I will take you in right now for resisting arrest."

Danny knew the fix was in and shut his mouth. It was going to be *yes sir* and *no sir* from here on out. He prayed that he had the recorder going. It sounded like he was going to need it. The captain was having trouble setting up the field breathalyzer. It was apparent he had very little exposure to arresting drunk drivers. Danny did smell of gin that was on his clothes, not down the hatch. That smell probably made the captain totally confident that Danny was drunk. No need for the balance test when the machine was all he needed. Finally, he put the unit together and held it up to Danny. "Blow, sweetheart."

"Sir, you have to show me that the breathalyzer is reading zero before you can administer the test."

"For a drunk with a gun you are pretty ballsy. You are going to get fired and maybe even do some time."

"Sir, I just want the proper procedure to be followed. Then whatever happens, happens." Danny's arms were at his side, and the right one was touching the cell phone. *Please let this thing be recording.*

The captain looked at the breathalyzer and turned it to Danny. He wasn't happy but knew that in just a few seconds he would be putting the cuffs on Danny and hauling him away. No department needs a drunk officer even if at one time he had been a hero.

Danny looked at the machine and the screen read, 00.000 just the way it should. Danny took a deep breath and blew until he heard the beep. The Captain snapped the machine away from Danny and expectantly read the screen.

"You're drunk," proclaimed the captain.

Danny starred at the captain in disbelief.

"You registered a point zero eight. Not much of a drunk, but drunk none the less."

"May I please see the screen?"

In triumph and with complete confidence, the captain pushed the breathalyzer into Danny's face. It took Danny a second or two before he could focus on the screen.

"Captain, I think you should recheck your screen. It isn't reading point zero eight. It is reading point zero, zero eight."

The captain turned the breathalyzer around and starred at the screen. After several seconds, he reached into his pocket and pulled out a set of reading glasses. He examined the reading on the screen looking back and forth from Danny to the screen. A look of surprise came on his face.

"You were at a party at the Butternut Brewery, weren't you?"

"Yes sir," was the professional reply.

"But you stink of gin."

"Yes, sir. I told you I had a drink spilled on me."

"Wasn't there beer in the backroom?"

"Yes, sir. But it was Bud, and I cannot stand Bud even if I paid for it."

"You do drink?"

"Yes, sir."

"Any other stops for DUI?"

"Only when I am the one doing the stopping."

"Ever been suspended for being drunk on duty?"

"I have never been suspended for anything." The captain's tone was changing. Danny was wondering about all these qualifying questions. The captain was now deep in thought. He eyed Danny up and down. Danny could see the wheels turning but had no idea where this was going. The captain could fake the test and just bring him in. It was his call and out of Danny's hands for the moment.

"You're the one who almost got cut in half from a shotgun blast." It was more of a statement than a question.

"That would be me. But he missed. All I got were a few scratches and a bump on the head."

The captain kept looking at Danny, then to the Butternut Brewery down the road, and then back towards Maidstone. He looked like he was trying to decide. In a much more conversational tone he asked Danny, "You have never been stopped for DUI?"

"No, sir."

For what seemed like a short lifetime, nothing was said. The captain was looking at Danny. His facial expression kept changing, but he didn't say a word. Finally, the captain got everything straight in his mind.

"Kid, sorry for the stop and the ball breaking. It seems I was misinformed, greatly misinformed. I want to apologize for my misunderstanding and the way I talked you. When you see Cornell, tell him to go fuck himself. No, no, don't do that. I will tell him to go fuck himself. I can get away with it. It would probably cost you your job and that is exactly what Cornell was looking for. I know we haven't gotten off on good terms with this little mess; but if you ever need anything from Great Barrington, you give me a call. Be careful."

He shook Danny's hand with a good solid grip. "I mean it," he said. The captain walked back to the cruiser and disappeared into Great Barrington. Danny pulled out the cell phone. To his surprise it was recording, and the voice quality of the stop on a silent night was excellent.

Chapter 27

"I was wondering when you would call. I figured it would have been last night," said Deverse.

"You heard the exchange between me and the captain from Great Barrington?" Danny asked.

"As soon as you hit the record button, everything was being transmitted. The FBI technical specialist got the tone that you had activated the recorder. I in turn got the call that you were in the process of being jammed up. I was getting ready to give Geri a call to get down to Great Barrington and bond you out. Nice job talking your way out. Now you need to explain to me how you spent four hours in a bar and came back a point zero, zero, eight. And who dumped the drink on you?"

"If the guy throwing the stag had not cheaped out and had Sam Adams or Heineken, I probably would have needed bail money. I guess Budweiser saved me. Then I would have been drinking, and it doesn't take much to get to point zero eight. Now, the gin is a whole different story. This bim from the big apple intentionally bumped into me and dumped a full martini on her and some got on me. She starts putting the moves on me, and I smelled a rat and got out of there. I found a nice hide spot where I could watch the bar and the parking lot and not be seen. Here comes Dolly Dimples making her way across the parking lot, and she is giving some guy holy hell on the other end of a cell phone conversation. She doesn't see me, but I can sure hear her. The gist of her tirade is that she was supposed to pick me up, but I split. She gets in her car and heads south. She was driving a New York registered Caddy. I waited for about an hour to see if anything else goes down, and when it looked okay, I headed for home. Right after I left the parking lot, the captain pulls me over. From there you know the rest."

"The captain for his part was set up too. He made a call to Cornell this morning. Then with a lot of very descriptive adjectives he read Cornell the riot act. It seems that Cornell told him that after the ambush you became unhinged and were out drinking every night and doing drugs. You had been stopped several times for DUI in other towns, but they all gave you a pass because you were on the job. Cornell was trying to get you the help you needed by getting the captain to stop you and make the arrest. Cornell would get you into a rehab program for your own good. After your run in, the captain saw things in a very different light."

"Now what?" asked Danny.

"Cornell tried to jam you up, and now a captain in a separate department knows that the fix is in on you. If Cornell makes another move, you have that captain in your corner to support your contention of a bag job. Throw your recorder in for good measure and the tape of the phone call this morning and you are golden. I don't think Cornell will try anything else, at least not right away. But he will be waiting for you to screw up. Always act like you know you are being recorded, sound and video. Always play to the camera even if one isn't there. Now give me that New York plate number, and I will run it. It will be interesting to see who it comes back to."

"Shit, I almost forgot;" said Danny. "After I got board-checked by the bim, she kind of talked me into buying her a replacement martini. She also had the bartender bring me a scotch. As we waited for the drinks, she starts getting a little overly-touchy-feely. You know, like crowding my space. She was rubbing up against me. All this happened in the first minute or so. She wasn't half bad, but up close you could see the heavy makeup, and the cigarette breath was killing me. The scotch and the martini came, and I looked around to see where I could make my exit. She raised her glass in a toast. I am about to take a good slug, and I saw flecks floating on the scotch. I make like I took a sip but didn't. Now I am totally spooked and know I have to get out of there. I tell her I have to check with the guys in the backroom and that I would be right back. Before she can protest, I am back in the stag room making for the back door with the scotch."

"Did you dump the scotch?"

"No. I put it in a hole in a cinder block that was being used to anchor the awning. I took some paper and tucked it in the hole to hide it. Do you think you can get someone to retrieve it and find out what was in it?"

"I am heading out the door right now. I will give you a call when I find out what we have."`

The line went dead. Danny had almost forgotten about the scotch. What the hell else can happen? Cornell, the lazy station rat that he was, could not have been doing this on his own. He had no connections and rolled over for everybody he perceived to have authority. It has to be Quenton or someone associated with Quenton. Cornell could not find a hooker like that.

Chapter 28

"Danny, a quick update. I did find the glass right where you said it would be, and there does appear to be something added to it. There is some sediment that is now resting on the bottom of the glass. I am shipping this off to the lab in Quantico, and we should hear back soon."

"That's great news; let me know the details."

"Not so fast. I did some checking on the captain from Great Barrington. He hates cops that drive drunk with a capital *H*. While you were away in the sandbox, his daughter was hit head-on by a totally shitfaced state trooper and killed. That night the trooper was leaving a retirement party when the accident happened. And this wasn't the first time he was caught driving drunk. Word got back to the captain that the trooper's bosses and several PDs were well aware of his frequent drunk driving and did nothing about it. All Cornell had to do was put a bug in his ear that you were doing the same thing, and he shows up doing a patrol check the night of the stag. He only stopped one vehicle all night. When he cleared from your stop, he went home. Next morning Cornell got an ear full."

"I guess that means I am on the wagon anywhere near town at least until this gets resolved," said Danny.

"That would not be a bad idea given all the possibilities. They might even set you up with a brake job and claim you rear ended the other vehicle. You already know how easy it is to spike a drink. One more thing, I have an electronic countermeasure guy available this afternoon. I want him to scan your vehicle for bugs or tracking devices. Drive down to Butternut Basin Ski Area and take Bear for a walk around five today. Anyone working there will be leaving around that time, and our guy won't stand out. It will look normal. He will have a backpack on that will hold the scanning equipment. Even if he gets a reading, he won't have to go near your vehicle. If he does, I will get back to you. Either way, I will get back to you."

"You really think they would spend that kind of money to track me?" asked Danny.

"Trust me, its dirt cheap and all done through cell phones and satellites. If it is Quenton, then he already has the means. Every one of his vehicles has that kind of transponder attached to it. If this were ten years ago, the device would have been a square foot, or so, wired in to the vehicles electrical power. These days it isn't much bigger than two quarters glued together. Depending on your location and the number of satellites visible to the unit, they can pinpoint you down to nine feet."

"That's not very comforting when you think about it. Big brother is here and watching your every move. I have been making my moves thinking that someone would have to be following me, and now you tell me all they need is a cell phone and one of those tracking apps."

"Pretty much, that's it," said Deverse, "but first things first. Get down to Butternut and take Bear for a walk. Then we can see if you are being tracked or bugged. Bugging is a little more difficult seeing that you have to get inside to have decent audio."

140

"You do remember the Jeep is a soft top, and I have the top down every day that it is good weather. Now if I am working or out where someone might go through the Jeep, I put the top up. But if I am just around town going shopping, then the Jeep is wide open."

"Shit! From now on if you are not in the jeep, keep it closed up."

"Got it."

Danny parked the Jeep off to the left and made his way up Butternut Ski area. Bear was right there checking out the spots where every other dog had been. The grassy ski slope was an easy but steady uphill hike. There were still a few cars in the parking lot. Some were ski area workers, and others were just like Danny--out to get some fresh air before dinner. Well, not exactly like Danny as he was pretty sure no one else would be having their vehicle swept for bugs. Danny had just made it to the top when his FBI cell phone rang. Now what?

"Danny," said Deverse on the other end of the line, "you have been bugged. The techy found a GPS device under the rear of the Jeep held on by a magnet. He took it off and it is sitting on your back bumper under the spare tire. What I want you to do is find a rough back road on your way home and drop it on the side of the road. That way when the signal stops moving, they will go out and look for it. They should be able to find it seeing that it will give them a nine-foot square box to search. This way it will look like it just fell off, and we didn't find it."

"How long do you think I have been tracked?" Danny wanted to know.

"The techy couldn't really tell, but he did say it wasn't very dirty, so he didn't think it was there for very long. On a good note, he did not find a recording device for audio

141

anywhere on the Jeep. So, go head to the Jeep and find a bumpy road."

"Now I have to assume that the Jeep at some point will be re-bugged. From now on, I have to plan where to park and what to do thinking that they, whoever they are, will be tracking my every move. If I go do some research at a library, I have to park far enough away so that they can't make the association of me to a location."

"Most of the time it isn't going to matter unless they are trying to set you up like at the brewery the other night. But, yes, they will know your location and every move in real time if they put another tracking device on you. If, for example, we need to meet and it is going to be in Great Barrington, you could park the Jeep near the restaurant on Railroad Street. You could go in, have a drink or just walk around, and then head down to the town green by a side street. The assumption will be that you are in the restaurant. When we are done with the meeting, you can go back in to the restaurant and kill some time before you go to the Jeep. While they can track the Jeep in real time, they can't follow you every time you go out for groceries or to have dinner."

"Sounds like a plan," and he hung up.

Danny and Bear made their way down to the Jeep. When Danny popped open the back door, he saw the tracking device right where it should be. Danny picked up the round object and hoisted Bear into the back. He slipped the tracker into his pack and headed for the exit. Just as he hit the exit, the FBI phone rang. Danny stopped at the turn around just outside the exit and walked away from the Jeep before answering the call.

"What now?"

"Do you still have it?" Deverse wanted to know.

"Yes, I just left the parking lot."

"Plan B. Keep the device in the Jeep for now. Do not, I repeat, do not drop it off like we planned. We are going to try something else. We are going to set up a time and place in the next day or so where you are going to drop it on the ground. We will have the location under surveillance and video whoever comes out to retrieve it. If it's a big fish, then we have a federal charge right there to nail him. If by chance it is a small fish, then we have some serious leverage to flip him. Either way, we are going to get somebody."

"Will you take them down right there?"

"The quick answer is no. We want to see who it is and get some background on the specific person. For all we know, they might send out one of the security people or someone with no connection to anything illegal. In that case popping him at the scene wouldn't help us but it would let them know that we knew they were tracking you. From time to time we will have the techy screen the Jeep just to see if they try again."

"If at some point we don't catch them, I really don't see a future here for me. This can only go on for so long. The FBI is not known for taking on cases that they can't win. Most of the time you guys only show up when you see a slam dunk."

"Realistically you are right. The big bosses saw this as an easy win with more people in the PD and the court system being part of the criminal enterprise that Snyder had been running. After months of investigation and wire taps with nothing coming up, they started removing agents from the case. Now the investigation is looking at the money aspect of the crime. But no one knows what that might be. We do have the payoff to Snyder to bag the case. Now having said that, without finding more people involved with Snyder, this case is not a big priority anymore. Widespread corruption would be, but the Bureau isn't finding that. That incident with the

Great Barrington captain has bought us more time. The fact that you almost got killed because of the FBI, the higher ups are letting the case run. If they hadn't tried to kill you back then, this case would have been over a while ago. We just didn't find the vast conspiracy that we thought was going on up here."

"What about the tankers I found and the fact that someone is wired into the new chief? There has to be something there. The call about me walking around a vacate greenhouse complex in the middle of the night. That is what you are supposed to do on a midnight shift, look around."

"True, but you looked around, took pictures, and came back off duty. That part made them nervous. I am pretty sure that the person who called was Quenton Worthington. Once the voice analysis is done, we will know for sure. The assumption when I brought it up is that they are using lower taxed home heating oil as diesel fuel for trucks. The kicker is that all home heating oil has a dye in it to identify it from truck fuel. The truck inspection guys are hot on that and pull a test sample on every truck they stop or that goes through the inspection station. So far Quenton's trucks have never been caught with fuel that had dye in it. How many of the big tankers have you seen going out to the greenhouse?"

"There is no way I can give you an exact number. First off, I don't work every night. There are nights I might be on a call and not in that area. If the trucker comes earlier or later than what the shift is, I would never see him. I do see the trucks headed out there from time to time. There isn't anything out that way that would take a tanker load that size. It isn't a thru road truckers would normally take. The smaller tankers are all over the place making home deliveries, so it is anyone's guess if they are going to the greenhouses or to a home for a delivery. The guy I stopped really did seem lost and glad that

I gave him the directions. If he were in on something criminal, I don't think he would have liked seeing a cop at that time of night."

"Well, keep an eye out and note the trucks and times you do see them. Things like this, even criminals like to keep a schedule. Maybe we can come up with a pattern. I will call you when we are set for the drop." Then the line went dead.

Chapter 29

Danny reflected on his recent past. In two situations just days apart, he could have lost his job, or someone might have tried to take him out. Wandering what he thought was a ghost town of a greenhouse complex, he was watched the entire time, day and night. If he hadn't had the two cell phones, the chief would have found the incriminating pictures he had taken and that might have set the wheels in motion. Then there was the stag party. Fortunately, the Butternut Brewery was an old collection of farm buildings with lots of rooms and exit doors. Had Danny been the typical cop, he would have been downing beers all night to get his money's worth. If that had been the case, then the Great Barrington captain would have nailed him for drunk driving. That would have been the end to Danny.

There was Dolly Dimples banging into him in the bar as he tried to disappear. If he had downed that scotch, who knows what might have happened--drunk, passed out in the parking lot where the captain would find him. Trying to drive drunk, the captain would have him the second he left the lot. Or the Bim takes him out back, and there are compromising photos or maybe the allegation of rape. It was only shit luck that he skated on all situations.

At that point Danny swore off drinking forever or at least until all this was over. He fingered the FBI cell phone in his pocket, he checked to see that the battery level was fully charged. The phone would stay at almost a full charge because Danny seldom used it. He checked the signal strength and noted he was at two dots. Not a strong signal, but good enough to make or receive calls. Photos could be a problem. He began practicing activating the recorder based on the button codes Agent Deverse had given him. He practiced for a while looking at the face of the phone to make sure he was getting it right. Each time he would do a recording test to see where on his person the recorder would get the best audio quality. Confident in his ability to activate the recorder without looking, Danny placed the phone in his pocket where he normally kept it and continued testing. Then the cell phone rang.

"Out of the house, now," ordered Deverse.

Danny shut the phone off and headed for the door.

About 100 yards from the barn, the phone rang again.

"What the hell is going on?" Agent Deverse demanded. "The audio techs are shittin a brick. They keep getting the emergency signal from you that you are recording with the phone, and then the line goes dead. They think you are in real trouble and are about to call the state police. Fortunately, in one of the recorded conversations they hear, *TEST*. So instead of calling out the cavalry, I was called. So, I ask you again, what is going on?"

"I'm sorry. The night I recorded the Great Barrington captain I wasn't sure I got it right until it was all over. I was practicing making sure I could activate the recorder without looking at it. Then I put the phone in various pockets to check where the best audio was. After that, I played it back to check the sound quality. Things are getting hairy, and I don't want to make a mistake."

On the other end of the phone there was a great sigh of relief from Deverse. "Next time you want to do some in-service training, let me know please. The transmissions were somewhat broken, and at times you said strange things that made you sound like you were in trouble."

"Well let me buy the guy a case of beer or scotch or whatever to make up for causing him all this grief."

"In this case it's *her* not *him*. I don't know the address they use at Fort Huachuca. I don't even know the name. Forget the beer and just keep in mind we are listening, and the other guys might be doing the same thing."

Shit, thought Danny. "Sorry for the trouble."

"On a positive note, I do have some information," said Deverse. "The name of the registered owner of the Caddy is definitely mobbed up. The guy's name is Anthony Carl."

"That does not sound like a mob name to me."

"He changed his name to Carl from Carlozzi so he wouldn't sound too Italian. He also made sure that everyone called him Anthony and not Tony. Even with the name change, he is still known to his friends and associates as Tony (two tires) Carlozzi."

"What's with the two tires?"

"Any time a problem had to be addressed, he made sure that when he ran a person over, he made contact with at least two tires. That was/is his trademark. He works out of Albany for the union and for the mob."

"Is he with the teamsters?"

"Kinda, he is with the freight division of the Teamsters Union. The freight guys and the Teamsters are two different groups with separate contracts, but the money goes into the same pool. They cover the guys working on the loading docks, and the head of the Teamsters is the head of the freight division."

"So, how does this connect to me?"

"It all points back to Quenton. He deals with these guys every day. When there is a problem, Quenton does not sit down with the local union rep, he gets to speak with the top guys at the union hall. Now Quenton's attorneys will sit down with the local representative, not Quenton. There can be walkouts and strikes, even some people getting fired; but in the long run, everything that happens is agreed to beforehand. No one wants to lose money with a strike or walkout. Each side figures out what they can afford in a dispute. Quenton needs to keep his trucks moving, and the union does not want the cost of strike pay. Strike pay doesn't amount to very much, but the teamsters don't want to lose any money. Once the union goes on strike, there is no way to get that money back plus they are not getting union dues. Strikes are a lose, lose situation for the unions. They do have to sound like they are standing up to the man, but at the end of the day they need to keep a positive cash flow."

"So, what do we do about Quenton?"

"Nothing right now. We know he is dirty and that he tried to set you up, but at this point he hasn't crossed the line. Much of what we have would turn into *he said, she said*. Asking that you get stopped for drunk driving is not a criminal charge. At least it is not a federal charge. We do not have a good chain of evidence with regard to the spiked scotch, and we can't say for sure who put the drugs in there. The scotch was left unattended for several hours. It could always be said that it was spiked during that time frame. We are getting there, but it will take time. More players are showing up."

The conversation ended without solving any problems except Danny had to stop playing with his cell phone.

Chapter 30

Danny was getting a bit paranoid thinking just about everyone was after him. In reality, it was only one or two people. Unfortunately, those one or two people were making his life miserable. Quenton wanted his ass for getting his son arrested for murder, a case that had already been taken care of and should have been a distant memory. Now the Worthington family had to fight this all over again. Because of Danny, a quiet and unfortunate suicide was now a murder. Brad Worthington, with the help of his new love interest, was trying to plead not guilty by reason of insanity. Knowing Brad and his temper, it just might work. Danny could understand why Quenton was after him but not Acting Chief Cornell. Why would Cornell stick his neck out for Worthington? Could a house in the woods be the sole motivation? Then the call came from Geri. Working the Organized Crime Task Force had been a good assignment. The downside was that they operated out of Fort Devens, a two-hour drive from Maidstone. Most of the O.C.T. operations were in the greater Boston area with some assignments a little closer in Springfield. Geri usually had weekends off. With Danny working midnights and getting rotating days off, whole day visits were few and far between. The visits were about to end.

Danny recognized the number on the cell phone, and a smile came to his face. "And how is the lovely state trooper doing these days?"

"It is no longer state trooper. You may now call me detective."

"Outstanding! What is your assignment going to be or are they going to keep you at Devens?"

"That's the downside," Geri said, and her voice got soft and no longer positive.

"Don't tell me they are moving you further east into Boston to work?" Danny's voice now had a worried tone.

"No, not Boston. A little further east than that."

Danny was now totally confused. "Geri, there isn't anything further east than Boston except maybe Cape Cod. You're not getting assigned to Bourne Barracks, are you?" The idea of adding one to two more hours to see her was depressing, and it hadn't even happened yet.

"I am being assigned to Interpol with a desk in Scotland Yard."

Danny gave a sigh of relief. "That's a good one, Geri. You had me going for a while there."

"Danny, I'm serious. I am being transferred next month."

Danny stared off into space. The one person he could trust was off on a European vacation. "Please tell me you are kidding."

"I wish I were, but this is no joke. I will get to come home several times a year, but for most of the time I will be in England or Ireland."

"Coming home a few times a year? How long are you going to be assigned to Interpol?"

"It's a two-year assignment." The answer was almost whispered. The phone was silent as both let the news sink in. Danny had so many thoughts that he couldn't even think of

151

something to say. All he knew was that Geri was leaving, and he was going to be in the Berkshires alone without a friend in the world. After the shooting and everything that followed, Danny had distanced himself from everyone but Geri. He wondered if this was set up by Cornell or maybe Quenton called in a favor just to stick it to him. Old man Worthington had his connections; he could pull this off.

"Why you?"

"They tell me that they liked my research work. Here I am banging on a computer and finding answers and connections that others had missed. They also like my last name."

"What the hell does your last name have to do with it?"

"My last name isn't Meehan, Brady, Bergin, or Cavanaugh. I am also not from the Boston area. Most of my targets are going to be leftovers from the IRA."

"There hasn't been a problem with the IRA in years."

"The answer to that is *yes* and *no*," Geri went on. "The running guns and funding for the IRA revolution was pretty much over. That left a bunch of people out of work. Some still supported the terrorist group, but others moved into drugs and smuggling weapons to groups like ISIS. They were doing the same things they did before just with a different customer. The Commissioner did not want anyone with an Irish background or anyone who had lived in Boston. After all the problems with Whitey Bulger, they were not going to walk down that road again."

Danny was listening but not really hearing. "I am not sure what to say. This is so sudden. I am at a loss for words."

"There is one positive thing, but it is two years down the road. When I am done with this assignment, I get the pick of barracks, no questions asked. Can you hang in there with infrequent visits home? I get to fly home on air reserve flights out of Westover Air Force Base. No charge and the flights happen every week."

Danny was letting things sink in, trying to find a positive note. He did not like Geri leaving, but she did have a career. It was going well--going much better than his right now. Her assignment had to be right up there for being one of the best. Danny was hurt, but didn't want to lay a guilt trip on Geri. It wasn't her fault, and it wasn't because of their relationship. It was just part of the job that no one expects.

"Danny, are you still there?"

He had no idea how long there was dead air, but it must have been a while. "I am here. I am just trying to sort this out, and it's taking time. Let me see about taking some vacation time and heading out your way."

"Don't burn your sick days and vacation days right now to come over and see me. Stop over on your days off because I have to work each day to update and turn over my assignments with my replacements. I won't have any free time to take a day off before leaving."

"You said replacements, plural?"

"Yes, it seems I have been doing the work of three up here. Each trooper that I am training is getting one third of my assignments."

"Classic over achiever."

"Bite me!"

"See you soon," and Danny hung up.

Chapter 31

Danny was trying to find the positive in this situation. Try as he would, it wasn't coming. This is one less thing to worry about, but he wasn't worried about Geri in the first place. He would now be able to concentrate more. No, if he concentrated any more than what he was doing now, he would pop a blood vessel. He wouldn't have to drive all the way to Fort Devens anymore to see her. No, the Mass. Pike took him on almost a straight shot to Devens. No, there was nothing positive about this. Danny sat and ran through his mind what two years of separation would be like. He thought back to the Marine days when they would come back from a deployment or from a remote training site. The married guys would have someone waiting, and there would be the hugs and tears of husband and wife missing each other. There was also the fair share of divorces that awaited some returning Marines. Danny decided he didn't want to contemplate the possible outcomes, grabbed a beer, and headed for the patio. Bear was right there beside him.

Danny sat back and looked over the beautiful horse pastures and the mountains beyond. *How could things get so complicated? Get out of the Marines and go to school. Hey, let's play cops and robbers for a while. Now meet a lovely young lady and almost get cut in half by a shotgun. Catch the bad guys and get set up in retaliation. Finally have the one solid thing going, and she gets shipped away to England. At least it isn't Baghdad.* Danny was deep in thought when the FBI cell phone beeped.

"What's up?" asked Danny.

"Some possibly interesting developments," said Agent Deverse. "We put a drone up over the greenhouses for a looksee and might have found something.

"Like what?" Danny wanted to know.

"It looks like there has been some recent digging in the yard there. There appear to be two trench lines dug between the fuel tanks and the brick building. From the photos the drone sent back, you can't really tell for sure; but that's what it looks like."

"Could it be electrical?"

"I don't think so because we have exposed wires in the air to the tanks from the road and other wires going to the brick building."

"Maybe they are getting the place ready to reopen. Those greenhouses had been in full operation right up until Mr. Seward died, and the kids didn't want anything to do with the place."

"Danny, who would put close to one hundred thousand dollars of fuel into tanks and not use it? If you fill those tanks up and then don't immediately start using the fuel, you are wasting money big time. If it is bread on a shelf or hamburger, you have to keep it moving. You don't buy it then freeze it hoping for a better day. Leaving that much money sitting there does not make good business sense."

"I follow you. The complex does not show any other activity to get the place back up and running. Plus, we are headed into summer and heating the greenhouses wouldn't be necessary. If they did crank up the heat, it would only be a few degrees and not for many hours. We do have cool nights, but once the sun comes up, you wouldn't need the heaters."

155

"We are doing some other checking, and I will let you know how it turns out," said Deverse. "But I have some really bad news for you."

"Geri already told me."

"She told you about Cornell?"

"No, she told me about her being assigned to Interpol for two years."

"Shit! I hadn't heard about that. What I have for you has nothing to do with Geri."

"So, what is this bad news?"

"It looks like Cornell isn't leaving after all. You do not have a new chief coming."

"How the hell did Cornell swing that? I thought that the new chief just had to hire his own replacement, and he would be down here in Maidstone."

"That was the plan until the new chief got himself jammed up in his old department. It seems that the town up in New Hampshire found out that the chief had made several personal phone calls on his department cell phone. They gave him a written reprimand for misuse of town property. A phone call was made to Maidstone ratting the new chief out. A special town council meeting was called to discuss this major transgression, and it was decided that Maidstone would withdraw its offer. You will hear about it today when you go in to work. A second special town council meeting is going to be held in the near future, and Lieutenant Lincoln Cornell is going to be asked to take over the chief's job on a permanent basis. The crazy part is that the phone the chief in New Hampshire was using has unlimited calling and texting. His using the phone didn't cost the town a dime. But it was enough that the small-town politics up there had an excuse to reprimand him and show him who the boss is. Maidstone jumped on it, and here we are."

"Oh mother-fucker, I am so dead. I should just drop my gear off at the station and head to Bob Marshall School of Forestry. First Geri leaves and now numb-nuts will be staying."

"Even if you wanted to head to New York State you can't start until fall, and that is several months away. You need a job until then."

"With that amount of time to work on me, I can see how easy it will be to find a reason to fire me."

"Wait a minute," said Deverse, "if they think you are leaving in the fall, they won't have to find a reason to fire you. There might be a revenge aspect to firing you and ruining your life, but if they think they can be done with you in a few months that might work for them. If you lay off the greenhouses and lay low that could buy you, and the FBI, the time we need to make a case. Think about it."

"I am thinking about it, and I cannot think anything positive is going to happen in my life in the near future."

"Give it a try. Talk to someone who will make sure it gets back to the chief. Then we can judge the attitude. We should see a change almost immediately in some way if they go for it. Once it gets to the chief, I will bet you that there will be a meeting or phone calls or both. From there we will know if you are safe or if we need to rethink this plan."

"Can this get anymore messed up?"

"Of course, but let's see if this works. Cornell and Worthington both have a say in this. But Cornell thought that he had a slam dunk on you being the department drunk and that backfired on him. He isn't a gutsy guy and was shittin' a brick when the Great Barrington captain called. He is very gun shy about sticking his neck out. He wants to be friends with Quenton, but he will only go so far. He likes the easy way out; and with you headed to Saranac Lake, that would be the easiest route for him."

"I won't say you're right, but it does make sense. I'll give it a shot. I know a few people I could talk to, and it will get back to the chief before the hour is up."

"Soft pedal it. Don't get on a soapbox. Just tell them it is time to move on. You always said being a police officer was only a stepping stone to forestry school. If you keep that tone and theme, they will buy it."

"Okay."

Chapter 32

Danny took Special Agent Tom Deverse's advice. He came into roll call early and found a seat in the break room. In front of him was the school catalog for Bob Marshall School of Forestry. It was folded open to the freshman year classes. The name was clearly visible. Danny had the registration form and was filling it out. He had these for over two years and was just now putting pen to paper. People filed by going to the coffee pot and checking activity updates posted on the board. It was impossible for anyone to miss what Danny was doing without even asking. Even so, he did get asked the sixty-four-thousand-dollar question. Are you finally going off to school? Danny would nod his head and make some noncommittal statement like, the fall is coming, gotta make plans now. He didn't offer anything more than that.

Most people responded with a grunt at the most. One officer wished him good luck. In this case Danny was counting on luck. No, more like he was praying for luck. Too often an officer might get involved in something and be perfectly justified in his actions. Given enough time and spin, a creative person could turn that action into a major department violation that would get the officer fired and maybe even arrested. Officers are expected to get into confrontations. It is part of the job description. Fighting with a suspect trying to take them in to custody was a daily possibility. Using your night stick, Cap stun or Taser were all possibilities. When it would it be appropriate to use them was up for wide interpretation. Second guessing and stacking the review board to get a predetermined outcome could easily be handled by the chief.

Most officers liked Danny. A few were on the fence, but they all kept their distance. Everyone could see that there was no love lost between Chief Cornell and the junior patrolman. No one really knew why there was a problem, but they knew it existed. Those who liked Danny were not about to take sides between the chief and the new kid. Officers were assigned to town meetings and could see how well the town fathers got along with the chief. Danny couldn't help them, and the chief for sure could hurt them.

Danny went about his business on the road making sure that his trip log showed a decent amount of activity. Checking closed businesses, assisting disabled motorists, and going on foot patrol where he could be seen. It was his normal activity before, but now he was concentrating on not being a target.

Danny gave Agent Deverse at the FBI a call. "I think it's working," said Danny. "It's been just over a week since I filled out the application in the roll call room, and this morning as I was going off shift in walks Cornell."

"Yeah, so?"

"He smiled at me and said good morning. Any other time he would just look the other way and keep on going without a word. He wouldn't even make eye contact. This time it was almost a friendly greeting. Actually, it was a friendly greeting. I was so shocked I just nodded my head."

"Excellent! Now just keep that low profile a while longer. We are working with the U.S. Attorney to obtain search warrants for the greenhouse property and financial records for Chief Cornell and old Quenton Worthington. They keep

160

kicking the warrant applications back asking for more information. Going after a chief of police is not taken lightly. We have more than enough information to obtain a search warrant if this were a normal case. Because Worthington is so well connected and we are including the chief, they are not accepting probable cause. They want proof beyond a reasonable doubt. If this has any chance of blowing up, we won't be getting the warrants."

"I think the heat is off me for the time being. I am staying busy on patrol but not trying to start anything. Cornell doesn't like tickets being written especially if the person lives in or near town. Tickets generate complaints, and the chief has to answer the complaints. He does not like confrontation. So, I am being seen and accounting for all my time. I am not interacting with the citizens in a negative way."

"Sounds like a plan. As soon as I hear anything, I will give you a call. I know I don't have to remind you, but stay away from the greenhouses, Cornell's new home, and Quenton's trucking operation. Our techies have eyes on all three twenty-four/seven. So, there is no need for you to go near any of those places."

"How did you manage that?"

"We have bucket trucks rigged out like cable TV installers," said Deverse. "We don't even need a search warrant when they mount the cameras on the utility poles so long as they don't go on the property. It takes all of 10 minutes to mount the unit. It has all the features, pan and tilt, zoom, and even good quality in low light. There is even a FLIR capability so we can detect heat signatures even when there isn't enough light to see someone with the low light scope."

"That thing has Forward Looking Infrared capability?"

"Absolutely!"

"Big brother is here."

"Big brother has always been here. It just takes less time and with better results."

"Give me a call when something breaks."

"Roger that." The line clicked off.

Chapter 33

The heat was off Danny for once but that was the only positive thing going for him at the moment. In filling out the form to get the chief to lighten up, Danny began wondering if heading out to forestry school might be a real possibility. He loved his Berkshires, but the small-town politics was killing him.

While down in Quantico, Danny imagined a different Maidstone than the one he had left. There would be big changes in the department. The new out-of-town chief would be there to take over and clean up what was left. He had hoped that Geri would get reassigned closer to Maidstone. She did get reassigned all the way to London. That wasn't what he had in mind. The week Geri had to pack and get ready for the move was like going to Hospice waiting for someone who was terminally ill to pass on. Their time together was spent in almost complete silence. Neither of them was talking about future plans or anything of significance.

It was a depressing ride to the airport. A lot of things should have been said but weren't. There was one last hug and a kiss at the TSA checkpoint. And then the isolation began. Sure, there would be emails, and they could Skype. There wouldn't be any back rubs or sitting in front of a campfire. They couldn't head down to York Lake and watch the sunset. Danny was back to Bear as his only friend. He had already stopped any kind of socializing with the other officers. He just couldn't risk it. He used to hit the Butternut Brewery a couple of times a week to have a beer and dinner. If the game was on, he might hangout there for a couple of hours. It would be more than enough time for someone to imply that he was a drunk and a barfly. Hiking was one solution, and heading way out of town was another. But around town he had to be very careful.

Midnight patrol took on the same boring routine every night. There would be the occasional accident or heart attack. A citizen might call in a prowler in their backyard that would be a hungry raccoon going through the garbage. With Agent Deverse's instructions to stay away from the target locations, Danny didn't have much to do. He kept track of all the tankers that came through town and noted the ones that might be going to the greenhouses or Worthington's terminal. But he couldn't follow them to know for sure. At the end of shift, he would make a verbal report to Agent Deverse's voice mail and call it a day. That was until early one morning around 3 am when the FBI phone rang. Danny's first thought was that Deverse was up late. The second was that maybe something happened in England. Danny hopped out of the cruiser and put some distance between himself and the car radios before he answered the phone.

Before Danny could get a hello out, Deverse was screaming into the phone. "Get the fuck out of there right now."

"Get the fuck out of where?"

"I told you not to go to the greenhouse. Now get your ass outta there."

"I am not at the greenhouses. I have south patrol, and I am sitting watching a couple of skunks raid the high school dumpster."

Deverse was in a panic. "There is a cruiser in the greenhouse complex, and there is movement about three hundred yards away. It appears to be human. The camera is over 400 yards away, and the techie is picking up on the FLIR and can't see much except the moving heat signature. Get on the radio and get him outta there now."

Danny dashed back to the cruiser. It had to be Gary Carlson. He had the central west patrol that would take in the area of the greenhouses.

"Unit Two," said Danny. "This is Unit One. Can I meet you at the Black Dog parking lot? I have to run something by you."

"Roger," was the clipped response.

"He's not moving," said Deverse. "He is still sitting there, and the FLIR still has the subject moving towards the cruiser."

"Unit Two, are you headed my way?"

"Roger."

"He is still not moving. Shit! He just put the cruiser in park and is getting out." Before Danny could say anything, Deverse nearly came through the phone. "He's taking a fucking leak. The FLIR has the object moving faster towards the vehicle. I think he saw him exit the cruiser. Screw it. Tell him to get out now and why."

"Gary, get out of there now, there is a guy coming up on you from your seven o'clock position."

Gary stared into the darkness, but saw nothing. How the hell would Danny know there was a guy out there? Gary figured it was some kind of a joke and continued on with his watering job. He didn't respond to the radio; he had his hands full.

"Danny, you have got to get him out of there. The FLIR shows the person has something long and dark in his hands. The object isn't showing any heat like the body is. No clue

165

what this guy's plans are, but he is moving up on an armed police officer in the dark. It can't be good."

But Gary did turn in the direction he was warned about and shouted into the darkness. "Screw you, asshole. Can't you see I'm busy?"

Gary was just about finished when he saw the flash and heard the boom of a shotgun. For a second Gary froze as he heard the double O buck shot fly past him. In an instant Gary dropped to the ground and pulled out his Glock.

"Gary, did you hear me? Get outta there right now." There was no response. Gary had other things on his mind. He had never been shot at. But he knew it when he heard it. Gary put the cruiser between himself and where he saw the blast come from. From behind the cruiser, Gary eased up over the trunk and let go all fifteen rounds from his Glock. He even dry fired a few rounds not realizing the gun was empty.

"Gary's down behind the cruiser and returning fire," said Deverse. "From what the techie can see, it looks like the guy shot at Gary with something very big judging by the size of the muzzle blast. He only got off one shot, and he is still moving."

"I'm on my way, but it will be five minutes before I can get there." Then Danny shifted to the cruiser radio. "Unit Two has shots fired at the Seward Greenhouse. I am on my way. Send help." Danny dropped the mike and concentrated on driving.

In the dispatch center it was total confusion. They had monitored the radio traffic and were trying to figure out how Danny was reporting things miles away from where he was. There hadn't been any radio traffic from Gary about shots being fired.

"Unit One, Unit Two, what the hell is going on? Unit Two has not reported any shots being fired." Both units were far too busy to answer.

Gary put a full magazine in his Glock and chambered a round. He eased up once more, and this time he fired in a slower more deliberate manner spacing the rounds going out making a sweep of the area. He had fired about half the magazine when there was a second blast. One of buckshot pellets found its mark and gouged a trench down the side of Gary's head just above the ear. For a split-second Gary saw a cascade of stars and a burning pain. His only though was *the mother fucker just killed me*.

"Fuck you." Gary screamed and stood up and took deliberate aim where he saw the muzzle flash. About the fifth shot he heard a scream in the darkness. Gary figure he must have connected with at least one round. Not wanting to take a chance, he finished off the second magazine and reloaded with his third. Ducking down behind the cruiser he reached up and touched his head. Blood was running down the side of his face. His grey uniform shirt was turning dark red. He was thinking he didn't have much more time. He hoped he killed the guy who killed him.

Gary pulled the portable radio from his holster. In as calm a voice as he could, he spoke slowly into the radio. "Unit Two, shots fired, I am hit. I need an ambulance. The suspect may also be hit. Please send help."

Danny was driving like a mad man trying to get there before it was too late. Deverse cut into his thoughts. "Danny, we have Gary sitting next to the cruiser holding his head. He got off a shitload of rounds, and the FLIR has the subject on the ground not moving. Whatever the mutt was firing, he got off two rounds. After Gary's last string of rounds, he stopped moving forward. He is also not pulling back.

Dispatch was getting a clearer but confusing picture. Units were on the way as well as an ambulance. Phone calls were being made. Officers were being ordered in. And Danny being the closest was still a minute away.

"We do not have any movement by the suspect." Deverse gave an update. "Gary is not moving."

As Danny roared into the complex, he spotted the cruiser with Gary resting up against the rear tire. He gave no indication that he heard the cruiser come in. Danny feared the worst as he rolled out of the cruiser and ran over to Gary. "Is the shooter still down?" Danny called to Deverse.

"Roger, no movement. How is Gary?"

As Danny drew closer, he could see that Gary was holding his bloody hand to the side of his head. The Glock was still clutched tight in his other hand. Then he noticed Gary's lips were moving, but he wasn't saying anything.

"Gary, are you okay?"

"Does it look like I'm okay?"

"Who are you talking to?"

"I'm fucking praying. You gotta problem with that? I'm praying that I don't bleed to death."

It was the first time Danny had ever heard Gary drop the F bomb. Danny switched on his flashlight, and gently pulled Gary's hand away to check out the damage. With all the blood, it was impossible to tell if the slug went in. Danny made a quick dash back to the cruiser for his first aid kit.

"Where the hell are you going? Don't leave me here to die alone."

"I am not leaving you. I have to get the first aid kit to patch you up and stop the bleeding." Danny tucked his flashlight into his neck and began to wipe away the blood. Gary was still bleeding at a good rate, but after several passes with a four by four topper sponge bandage, Danny could see that it was a grazing wound. The slug had not entered the skull. From the first aid kit, Danny retrieved a quick clot packet and poured it into the wound. Next, he took several four by fours and pressed it on top of the wound. "Give me your left hand and hold the pads in place while I wrap your head. You are not going to die, but you will have an awesome scar. The chicks are going to love it when you tell them how you got it."

"Fucking jarheads and their scars. Some bedside manner you have. Look at all this blood."

"The quick clot worked. I don't see any new blood coming from under the bandage." Sirens could be heard heading their way. Now to find the shooter. Danny spoke into the FBI cell phone. "Is the shooter still holding in place?"

"Roger that, no movement at all."

Gary looked up at Danny, "Who the hell are you talking to?"

"Long story, maybe later."

Chapter 34

"Okay," said Danny into the phone, "walk me into the guy." Danny moved out. The flashlight was off and stowed in his side pocket. The Glock was pointed towards the woods. His left hand was holding the cell phone getting directions and distances to his target. He moved slowly and as quietly as possible. He didn't speak into the cell phone. While he was walking, the cell phone was giving him a constant update on his progress and that his target was not moving. The sirens from the responding units covered the noise of his footsteps. Finally, he was fifteen yards from his target. It was still pitch black; and while Danny knew right where the guy was, he still couldn't see him. Danny took a deep breath, show time.

Danny eased the cell phone into his pocket and switched on the flashlight. "Freeze, asshole." The suspect flinched at the roar of a command and tried to hide from the light. The suspect had a gaping wound to his right knee. Blood was pumping from both sides. The mutt was doubled over in pain with his hands trying to stop the bleeding. Good shot, thought Danny. In the pitch black ole Gary connected. About a foot away was a sawed-off double barrel shotgun. That would be fine for close in, thought Danny, but at anything over 50 yards was anyone's guess where the pellets might go. Danny kicked the shotgun away and kept his Glock trained on the suspect.

"You screwed up big time, sweetheart," Danny pointed out. "That was supposed to be me down there." The man wasn't paying much attention to Danny. He was in tremendous pain and knew he was bleeding to death.

"You have to get me to a hospital. I need medical attention, or I am going to bleed to death. Get me down to that ambulance now."

"First things first," said Danny. "Who hired you?"

"Screw you--get me to a hospital. I know my rights."

Danny stepped up to the suspect and stuck his Glock in the mutt's mouth. Danny shoved it in so far, the suspect gagged. He let go of his leg to reach up for the gun but just as quickly went back to squeezing his knee to stop the bleeding. "You have the right to remain silent," said Danny. "If you do choose to remain silent, it just might take a while for the ambulance to makes its way up here. If by chance you do manage to scream for help, then I will have no choice but to pump a few rounds into you and place the shotgun in your dead hands. Now you don't look too good. The color is draining out of your face. I suspect you are getting lightheaded and cold on this nice warm evening. Am I right so far?" Danny twisted the Glock ever so much so that it would remind the mutt of where it was just in case the pain got to be too much.

"Now, let's try this again. Who hired you, and what is your name?" Danny eased the Glock out ever so slightly so that the mutt could mumble an answer.

"Fuck you." And the Glock went halfway down his throat.

"Wrong answer, bucko. You only have a few minutes left before you go unconscious, and then you won't be of any value to me. At that point I will give it another minute or two to make sure you have bled out, and then I will be screaming

171

for the EMTs to get up here because I just found you. Tick tock, sweetheart. What's it going to be?"

Danny could see panic in the suspect's eyes. Every few seconds Danny would look at his watch just to reinforce that valuable time was slipping away. "You are getting more and more light headed and somehow getting colder. One way or the other, we will find out who hired you. The question you have to ask yourself is will you still be around. Right now, the way things are going, you won't be. Besides, would this guy stand up for you if the tables were turned?" Once more Danny looked at his watch and shook his head. "Not looking good for you at all. Hell, it might already be too late."

Terror filled the suspect now realizing that Danny wasn't bluffing and that he had better start talking fast if he wanted to see tomorrow. It might be in a prison cell, but it would be better than bleeding to death.

"Tony C. from the union hired me. I think his last name Carlozza or Carlonzi or something like that. He said a guy who owned a trucking firm wanted this dump protected. I made three hundred a night just to sit here. He promised twenty-five thou if I blew away a cop. For the life of me, I never thought I would be shooting anyone."

Danny fished around in his pocket for the FBI phone and hit the record sequence. "One more time;" said Danny. I want to hear it again from the top. Who hired you?"

"What are you going to do about the bleeding?"

"I am on it, now talk." Danny open one of his belt pouches and pulled out a pair of gloves and long strap.

What's that?" the mutt wanted to know.

"Tourniquet kit. Now let me hear it again."

"You carry a tourniquet on your belt?"

"Yes, old habits die hard. Now who sent you?"

172

The mutt was talking as fast as he could and left nothing out. When Danny was satisfied, he wrapped the tourniquet around the mutt's leg and pulled. The mutt let out a deep groan. The pain was worse, but the bleeding immediately stopped. Danny called out to EMTs who were treating Gary back in the lot. Soon Danny was joined by several ambulance people, and they proceeded to pack up the shooter and get him down to an ambulance.

The greenhouse lot began filling with police cars. Danny looked across the compound and realized it was happening again. No one was taking charge just like the last time. It isn't going to be like the last time, Danny said to himself.

"Okay, "said Danny, "get Gary and the mutt loaded and then everyone gets back on the street. This is a major crime scene, and I don't want anyone messing it up. Danny spotted the new detective lieutenant and trotted over to him.

"You are the ranking officer right now. How about we freeze the scene? We need to start an entry exit log with everyone coming and going plus why they were here. Once we have the scene locked down, we can plan without the scene being compromised. This is probably going to a state police investigation, but of course that isn't my call to make."

With that last thought the FBI phone buzzed.

It was Deverse, and he seemed relieved. "Nice confession. Even if later he changes his mind, you have him recorded. Did anything else happen before you turned the recorded on? The images were not all that great, but you were with him for a while before the recorder went on. Then it was only after the statement that you began to work on him. What was up with that?"

"Just trying to make the location safe and confirm that he understood me."

"Did he understand you?"

"I got the statement, didn't I?"

"I guess I don't need to know any more than that."

Chapter 35

The arriving officers and detectives began the process of securing the scene. Everyone was checked for evidence and logged off the property. The detective lieutenant was on the phone pacing up and down. His free hand was going through the air like a knife slashing away at unseen object. Finally, the free hand made a final dramatic cut. He stared at the phone; and with enough force to push the off button four feet into the ground, he hung up. If the dark hair and thick mustache didn't give him away as being Italian, the hand sword gestures did.

"Dumb shit mother fucker," was all he could say.

"What's wrong LT?" Danny wanted to know.

"The chief wants us to process the scene right now. He has no intention of calling out the State Police Major Crime Squad. In his mind this is a simple case, and we have the suspect under arrest. We have the firearm. He wants the scene processed and cleared in an hour. There is no way we can do that. Just mapping the scene and marking off the evidence will take hours. Then we can start collecting the evidence. The scene isn't beyond our capability, but it is labor intensive. We don't have enough people. Between the cops, the firemen, and the ambulance, we have over 20 people to get statements from; and we need those statements before they start comparing notes. It just won't work."

"I have a suggestion for you," said Danny. "Get started with the scene being locked down and finish the entry/exit log. Buy me some time to make a phone call and maybe we can save the situation. Keep the guys busy so if the chief checks, you were following his orders to the letter. You already told him you needed more time."

"Is this going to turn in to a shit storm with me out front?"

"Just stay busy while I make the call. I will know in a matter of minutes one way or the other if we can get help on this."

The detective lieutenant nodded his head and with a heavy shrug, turned, and began giving orders. Everyone leaving the scene was to be interviewed separately. That will easily eat up an hour, he thought.

Danny pulled out his FBI phone. Deverse picked up on the first ring. "I got bad news, and I need some help," said Danny. He went on to explain the chief's directions and was doing his best to slow things down, but he didn't have a lot of time with the chief breathing down the detective lieutenant's back. True to form, Chief Cornell did not leave the station. But it would only be a matter of time before he would want an update and an estimated time for clearing the scene. He might even get a call from Quenton to get his ass down there to take care of things personally. By now they both must know that the hit man was wounded, and an arrest had been made. They didn't know what he said to Danny. Danny for his part wasn't talking about the statement either. The mutt didn't know he was being recorded; in his mind, he had time to make up a good story.

"The State Police Major Crime Squad is not coming out."

Danny exploded. "What the hell do you mean they aren't coming out? This case is as good as bagged if it is left to Cornell's direction."

176

"Relax. The FBI Crime Scene Units from Boston and Albany are on their way. We are asserting federal jurisdiction on this case. Cornell should be speaking with the Special Agent in Charge of the Boston Office right now. He is going to be told to freeze the scene, separate all witnesses, and to stop any investigation."

"But this is a totally local crime. There isn't any federal crime here. This isn't a bank robbery. How can you take over the case?"

"How does attempted murder of a federal officer sound for jurisdiction?"

"Bullshit. Gary isn't a federal officer."

"That's exactly what I think Cornell will be saying. Do you recall a time when a certain Maidstone police officer was sworn in as a Special U. S. Marshall and went on the federal payroll? The hit was directed at you even if Carlson was the one to get shot. Plus, you are the one who made the arrest, and you are a federal officer on the job. Hang on; I have a call coming in."

Deverse came back on after what seemed like a lifetime but was really less than a minute. "Get with the detective lieutenant and have him call Cornell if Cornell hasn't already called. He will have some instructions for Nanfito."

"Got it." Danny turned to where he last saw the LT. He was standing about fifty yards away and was on the phone. Danny couldn't hear what was being said but knew something had changed. The sword hand was down tight by his side. There were no hand gestures. The detective lieutenant was hunched over. Every few seconds he would nod his head. When the call was over, Nanfito looked at the cell phone and gently tapped the off button. In slow motion he slid the phone back into his pocket. He raised his head and squared his shoulders and let out a long deep breath. He surveyed the scene and then his gaze made eye contact with Danny. He gave Danny a long-appraised look. It was a look of disbelief. He then raised his hand up and gave a handshake of thumbs up. Danny returned the gesture. With that Detective Lieutenant Dominic Nanfito began issuing orders, and people began to move.

After getting things squared away, the detective lieutenant came over to Danny. "Who the hell are you connected with?" he wanted to know.

"Why, what happened?"

"I get this call from the chief. Except it didn't sound like the chief; it sounded like a bad recording. In this monotone voice, he tells me to stand down and hold the scene until the FBI gets here. When they do, I am to turn everything over to them and assist them in any way possible. I have to get two officers down to the hospital to babysit the prisoner. No matter what, an officer has to be with him at all times. He cannot have a visitor, not even an attorney. The FBI or the U.S. Marshall Service will be there to relieve them. He asked if I understood. I said, 'Yes, chief.' His response was, 'Yeah, chief for now.' What the hell does that mean, and who did you call with that much juice?"

"For the time being, let's say I made some connections down at Quantico. We shall see over the next few days what shakes out."

Chapter 36

The crime scene tape was up blocking off the greenhouse complex from the road. Officers were stationed at both ends of the street to keep vehicle traffic away. A lone officer was up on the hill where the shooter had been taken in to custody. Witnesses who actually participated in what went down were seated in cruisers parked just outside the crime scene tape. The excitement was gone, and the adrenaline had subsided. People were getting antsy to get on with everything from getting breakfast to going to work. And then the caravan arrived. No lights and sirens. No screeching brakes or clouds of dust, but it was impressive. The first vehicle was a big black Ford SUV. Four SWAT officers in full gear exited the vehicle, their M-4 carbines slug across their chests. The second vehicle was a gleaming black Ford LTD. Four agents exited the vehicle dressed like Wall Street bankers. Those two vehicles were followed by a crime scene van, a bus-like command post, and at least a half dozen Ford LTDs and SUVs. Within seconds the area was swarming with blue windbreaker FBI raid jackets. An agent from the first vehicle approached the crime scene tape and announced to the Maidstone officer controlling access that he was Special Agent Osborne Steinmetz, and he was now in charge of the crime scene.

"Who was in charge?" Agent Steinmetz inquired.

The officer gestured to Detective Lieutenant Nanfito.

"I need to speak with him now please."

The officer waved the LT over.

The agent held up his FBI credentials for the detective lieutenant. "We will be taking over the crime scene from here on. I need a full briefing on everything that has transpired this morning. I will have agents replace your officers, but I want them to stay on post until we have a full debriefing. You were briefed that this would be an FBI case, I hope?"

"Yes, I was told to hold the scene until you relieved me. Whatever you need."

"Good. Let's go over to the command post bus, and you can bring me up to speed," said Agent Steinmetz.

At that moment, a completely detailed Lincoln Navigator pulled up to the access point past all the other vehicles. An agent in the front passenger's side exited the vehicle and opened the rear door. A distinguished looking woman in her late 40s or so exited the vehicle. She, too, was dressed for Wall Street. From the moment the first vehicle had pulled in, no one took their eyes off the road and the flock of vehicles and FBI agents who had descended on Maidstone. Scenes like this didn't happen here unless word got out that Arlo Guthrie was in town. The lady approached the agents and officers at the access point. Special Agent Steinmetz made the introductions. No one had ever heard of U. S. Attorney for Western District of Massachusetts Dianna Sheriden. And that was the way she liked it.

Ms. Sheriden surveyed the scene searching for something or someone. Finally, she asked, "which one is Officer Gilcrest?"

Lieutenant Nanfito looked surprised but did not hesitate. He pointed across the compound to where Danny was standing near the damaged cruiser.

180

"That would be Danny over there in uniform," he said pointing across the compound.

"I need to speak with him. Could you have him come over? I don't want to enter the crime scene. Let's limit the people who go past the crime scene tape."

Then Nanfito spoke Danny's name into the portable radio. Hearing his name and recognizing the voice, Danny looked in the direction of the entry control point where there was now a gaggle of people. Danny had noticed the vehicles arriving, but his attention was concentrating on Gary's cruiser and the damage to it from the shotgun blast. He was estimating the distance from the shooter to where the vehicle and Gary were hit. The distance was so great that the double O buck had lost a lot of its velocity. But now his name was being called over the air. Nanfito lowered the portable and waved Danny over. He gave the cruiser one last look and then pulled out his FBI phone and snapped a few pictures. Danny would not be part of the crime scene processing, so chances were good that he wouldn't be on the inside of the tape much longer.

Danny made his way to the entry control point and logged out with the officer on duty. He then approached the detective lieutenant. At the same time several FBI Agents closed in on the U. S. Attorney, and they all drifted over to where Danny was now standing.

The LT gestured to the U. S. Attorney. "They want to speak with you, any idea why they picked you out?"

"No clue."

Dianna Sheriden walked up to Danny and extended her hand. "I am Dianna Sheriden from the U. S. Attorney's Office. I am in overall charge of this case now, and I am very pleased to finally meet you again. I am sure you don't recall the first time we met."

181

Danny racked his brain trying to remember where he might have met her but was coming up empty. The image that Ms. Sheriden presented was that of a perfectly dressed model for a female executive in some upscale store. From her hair to her shoes, everything was, in a word, perfect. Not a hair out of place. Not a speck of lint on her black outfit. She wore silver jewelry that was not over done but was very tasteful and complementary. The white shirt glowed under the black jacket.

"I am sorry, I do not recall meeting you before. I am sure if I had, I would remember." After saying that, Danny nearly choked at his sexist comment. She was a stunning individual that no one would forget. He was afraid she might not care for his comment, but instead she gave a small smile and thanked him.

"If you recall graduation day at Quantico," she began, "you came up on the stage and met the Director of the FBI and a representative from the Justice Department. You received your diploma and then the cameras kept snapping pictures of you, the Director, and the U. S. Attorney. Do you remember that day?"

As she spoke, Danny was taken back to Quantico and the special attention that was paid to him on stage--attention he wanted to avoid. "Oh yes, I remember that day. But once on stage, everything turned into a blur. I took my diploma and then started to exit the stage like everyone else. Of course, that didn't happen. But I don't recall meeting you there."

The crowd around Danny and Ms. Sheriden hung on every word, and Danny could feel the pressure. If Danny had met Ms. Sheriden, he should remember her, not only because of her position in the Justice Department but because of her stunning beauty.

"You were pretty occupied with the handshakes and photos to notice me. I was the one handing the diplomas to the director to give to you. I wanted to be up there on the line to congratulate you myself, but I was outranked by a more senior DOJ official. Still, it was an honor to be part of your graduation ceremony. Now we finally meet in person, and I can shake your hand and thank you for your service and dedication."

She held Danny's hand with a firm confident grip. Danny was surprised at the firmness from such an elegant Lady. Danny finally got his thoughts together and figured out he had to say something.

"Thank you, ma'am. I had a great time down there at the academy."

Chapter 37

Ms. Sheriden turned to Special Agent Steinmetz. "Ozzie, don't we have something for Officer Gilcrest?"

Danny nearly choked on his last breath. Now every eye in the crowd was bouncing like pinballs between the lovely DOJ attorney, an FBI special agent, and a police officer who looked like he was ready to run. *What could they possibly have for me? This whole thing just went down. What the hell is going on?*

Special Agent Steinmetz stepped forward and handed Ms. Sheriden a long black leather billfold. Across his arm was a navy-blue jacket. Ms. Sheriden took the wallet in a most reverent move holding it as if it were delicate and needed to be handled gently. She turned the leather case over in her hand and a gold star appeared. With both hands she held it out to Danny. For a moment he hesitated, not sure what to do.

"You have already been officially on the job," she began. "Now it is time for you to start working in the open. As the spies say, come in from the cold." She placed the U. S. Marshall shield and credential case in Danny's hands.

Taking the case, Danny gazed at the U. S. Marshall shield and slowly opened the credential wallet to see his FBI National Academy face starring back at him on his own U. S. Marshall identification. It was all there, completely official. Before Danny could say a word, Agent Steinmetz stepped forward and handed Danny a U. S. Marshall raid jacket. Danny was at a complete loss, not sure what to say or do. For a moment everyone stood around waiting to see what would happen next. Most everyone in the circle was looking at Danny. Things had ground to a standstill, and Ms. Sheriden stepped up and took charge.

"Everyone here is on the clock, and we have a lot to do," she said. "So how about putting your credentials away, putting your jacket on, and getting with Agent Steinmetz to bring him up to speed." With that Ms. Sheriden turned and headed for the Lincoln Navigator. But something crossed her mind. Without a thought to whom she might offend, she abruptly turned and addressed Danny. "Is there anyone here right now that we should exclude from this investigation?"

Danny hesitated for a moment and let the question sink in. Yes, there were people he didn't trust in the department. Some he didn't trust a little but others a whole lot. Danny looked at the closest police officer, the detective lieutenant. The look back from the LT was one of surprise and dreaded anticipation. Danny moved on looking over the compound. As he came to each officer, he hesitated for a moment. Days and weeks of memories flooded back as he looked at each face and searched his brain for conversations or actions he could remember for each person. His search was slow and methodical. There would be no rushing. Ms. Sheriden for her part made no effort to speed things up. Quietly she was appreciating the internal assessment Danny was making of each and every officer.

The behavioral guys down at Quantico were right, she thought. This is one good cop and a real leader. Cool under pressure. Give him a tough question, and he will give you the best-informed answer. Even with his detective lieutenant standing right there, he looked him up and down not intimidated by his rank or seniority. A smile slowly came across Danny's face as he completed his assessment.

"Everyone here is fine. All good stand-up guys. Not too many outspoken ones, but who came blame them for not wanting to commit department suicide standing up to the chief."

"Excellent," said Ms. Sheriden as she made her way to the vehicle. As she entered, she called out, "Oz, you got this. Anything you need just call. If Danny suggests or tells you something should be done, do give it serious consideration."

"Aye, aye, ma'am," was the response from Agent Steinmetz.

Danny turned to Agent Steinmetz and asked, "Jarhead or Squid?"

"Jarhead"

"Who were you with?"

"EOD"

"Let me see your hands."

Up came Agent Steinmetz's hands. He smiled and displayed all eight fingers and both thumbs. "Close more than a few times, but I am a quick little bunny when it comes to getting blown to shit."

For the first time Danny thought that this was going to turn out okay. "Agent Steinmetz, what's next?"

"Please don't call me Agent Steinmetz. I have any number of nicknames that work better. Unless I am trying to be overly officious, I don't use the agent title. The boss calls me Oz, but the guys call me the Wiz, but not if I can hear them."

"So, what do I call you?"

"How about my Marine call sign?"

"And that would be?"

"Boom!"

"Oh shit."

"Hey, I still have all my fingers and most of my sanity. Let's get to work. Give me the rundown of what happened here."

"It isn't a bad start for your crime scene guys. Once we got the suspect and Officer Carlson loaded up, we got everyone out of the crime scene area. The detective lieutenant has been in a holding pattern waiting for you guys to show up and take over. We have a roster of everyone who entered the scene and why, along with all their contact information."

"Better than I had hoped; let's get the LT over here and get this show started. What is with the fuel tanks and that brick building? They look like the only things still intact."

"There is diesel in the tanks. There could be up to thirty thousand gallons of it. As far as the brick building goes, we have asked ourselves the same thing and so far, we haven't figured it out."

"Whom are you referring to as *we*?"

"Me and Agent Deverse."

"Ah, Obi Wan. Great."

"Obi Wan?"

"A long story. When it's Miller Time, I will explain." Agent Steinmetz waved a junior agent over. "Get a search warrant for the entire compound and make sure we get to enter that brick building. Get those magic creative fingers of yours working because we can't do much without the search warrant?"

"Aye, aye, sir"

"The Jarhead thing, it kinda caught on," said Steinmetz.

"I see."

It was going to be a long day. But unlike the last shooting scene in Maidstone, it wasn't going to be a mess.

Chapter 38

At this point there wasn't much for Danny to do at the scene. Interviews were being done by the agents, and Danny was working on his report after briefing Agent Steinmetz. For the first time, Danny felt like this was finally going to be over. They had the connection to old man Worthington. The down side was that there wasn't a link to the hit on Danny. The case interference was an open issue. Danny sipped his coffee as he worked on his computer. As the words appeared on the screen, he couldn't help but reflect on everything that had happened in the past few years since he left the Marines. Come home, take a few college courses locally, and then off to forestry school and a career in the woods. It had been a simple plan. No major details or things to accomplish. How in the world did he get in the middle of all this? Was it karma, he wondered? Would all of this still have happened if he had stayed in the Marines? He would never know because that was not the path he chose.

I better get back to the report or it will never get done. From time to time Danny would look up expecting to see Deverse pull in. But, so far, there was no Deverse. Or should I start calling him Obi Wan?

"Hey, Boom, where is Deverse?"

"Oh, he is having a little sit down with your chief."

"Is he interrogating him?"

"That would be *yes* and *no*. See, Obi Wan has his own way of doing an interview. First off, he asks almost no questions but gets a person talking. He has a way of keeping the person talking with gestures, nods, grunts, and just a few words. After a while, a person who was reluctant to talk can't be shut up. At that point, he still lets the subject run free and paint himself into a corner. That is, of course, if there is a corner to be painted into."

Danny thought back to his conversations/interrogations he had with Deverse. *It works*, Danny thought.

"When the subject thinks he has talked himself out of trouble and sits back in confidence, Obi Wan, in a quiet and gentle voice, proceeds to take the subject apart one tiny piece at a time. When Obi Wan starts, it seems he is just looking to clear up a few minor details. The subject is completely willing to help out thinking that just a few more words will help make this all go away."

Boom went on. "The first time I watched him do an interview that was recorded, I couldn't believe he was going to get a confession. I watched, I don't know how long, as the subject being interviewed ran the show. The subject, not Deverse, was in complete control. As the minutes ticked by, the subject got more confident; and his body language shouted out that he was in complete charge. He was beating this FBI agent at his own game. Then Deverse made his move. No yelling. No finger pointing. No accusations. Just a tired, old, slightly overweight over-the-hill FBI Agent, trying to wrap things up and be on his way to lunch. You heard things like, 'Could you help me here?' or maybe, 'I think I got this wrong, what did you mean by...' Then he might use, 'Sorry, I think I missed something when you said....'

"As each one of these *help me* questions gets answered, it's not long before the body language changes. The subject slides

189

back in his seat. The arms begin to cross. Then the feet cross, followed by a full leg cross. The confident direct eye contact stops, and the subject is now staring at the floor with only an occasional glance up. The full first half hour of the tape seemed to drag on forever. As I watched, I knew beyond a shadow of a doubt that Deverse was not going to get a thing from the subject. The second half of the interview took forty-five minutes, but it seemed like five. The subject was toast. In the end, he gave it all up. Then to top it all off, he thanked Deverse and shook his hand."

At that very moment, Deverse was working his magic with Chief Lincoln Cornell of the Maidstone, Massachusetts Police Department. The chief's office was decorated in a manner befitting a chief of police of a very wealthy town. Some items were accidental antiques that had been in the town's possession for decades, handed down from the mayor's office to different departments. Some of those items would end up in the chief's office. Instead of being old hand-me-down furniture, they had become cherished collectable antiques. The prior chief had used almost all of the department's maintenance funds for one year to panel and carpet the room. His direction to the contractor was, "I want this place to look like the district attorney's office on *Law and Order*."

The chief got his wish. The room exuded confidence and stability. These were qualities that Special Agent Deverse appreciated. There was a feeling that it gave to the occupant, a superior feeling, everything that Special Agent Deverse looked for in an interview. When the hammer finally dropped, the confidence/over confidence would be the subject's downfall. If the occupant felt safe in his own personal palace, it was his undoing.

When the interview came to what Chief Lincoln Cornell thought was the end, he was riding on cloud nine. He had beaten the FBI at their own game. He showed them who was boss and ran the Maidstone Police Department. Chief Cornell stood up ready to show Special Agent Deverse the door. But Agent Deverse remained seated. Chief Cornell gave a questioning look to Deverse, but the agent remained seated.

"Take a seat," said Deverse.

Chief Cornell was about to protest with the excuse that he had a major case going on and needed to get an update. Agent Deverse removed a voice recorder from his pocket. Chief Cornell was taken aback.

"You recorded me without my knowledge!" he demanded.

"Yes," was the short reply. "Here is the warrant that authorizes me to make just such a recording," and he held it up for Chief Cornell to see. Then Agent Deverse hit the play button. It wasn't the recent conversation between the two of them. It was a phone call, hours earlier, between Quenton Worthington and the now wilting Chief of Police of Maidstone, Massachusetts--the soon to be ex-chief. Eventually, he would go on to be a federal prisoner. Deverse played the recording for several minutes. Chief Cornell stared at the little machine without blinking. As he listened to the recording devise, he saw his future life slipping away--the salary of a chief of police, a new, well-appointed office--all disappearing in a heartbeat. The home until just a few months ago that had only been a distant dream. The chief's new status as a person of power in Maidstone. As the recorder played, he saw it all go up in flames. A stunned chief sat back down in the oversized office chair, his face a total blank.

"You told Quenton you were going to take care of everything," said Deverse. "Just how were you going to do that?"

A blank stare was all that Chief Cornell could offer.

"Well, how were you going to take care of everything?"

In the voice a frog might make, he offered up all he had. "I don't know. I had to tell him something. I didn't want to disappoint Quenton and lose the house."

"One of your guys almost got his head blown off. You're going to figure out how to take care of Quenton because you don't want to disappoint him? Is Gary Carlson or Danny Gilcrist's life worth a house to you?"

"Everything was going so well until Danny came back. If he had just moved on, none of this would have happened. The town was just fine until he decided to stick his nose in where it didn't belong. If he had just left things alone--but no, the damn boy scout screwed everything up."

"I don't think the federal prosecutor will see it that way. Everything you said to Worthington has been recorded. Every phone call you made to him, every email. Think about the conversations you have had over the past few months. Think how that is going to sound to a jury."

"Aren't you going to read me my rights?"

"How about shut the hell up. I don't want to hear another word out of your sorry, greedy mouth."

Chapter 39

Things at the greenhouse complex were moving along in clear and efficient manner. Granted it was at a snail's pace, but nothing was being left out. After briefing Agent Steinmetz, there wasn't much for Danny to do but sit there and watch. The upside was that there was an unlimited supply of fresh brewed Eight O'clock coffee. The one thing Agent Steinmetz insisted on being include in the crime scene van was a 24-cup brewing machine and a good supply of Eight O'clock. Danny and Agent Steinmetz stood back as a welder from the Barnes Air National Guard Base cut away the lock on the brick building. A fire truck stood by with several hoses deployed. One fireman was providing a steady follow of water onto the lock area keeping any sparks down. No one knew what was inside, but everyone speculated that it had something to do with the fuel. Before the lock could be completely removed, a full-size tanker truck pulled up to the gaggle of police and FBI vehicles outside the gate. All eyes turned to the tanker.

"Think we should have a look?" asked Danny.

"Yes, but that truck is not included in the search warrant. We can't just go over and start searching it," said Steinmetz.

"I bet if I asked nicely, he would give consent. As far as we know, the truckers have no idea that anything is going on. The one trucker that I talked to was very glad to see me and thanked me for giving him directions."

"Won't hurt to ask, all he can say is no. Then we impound the truck and get another warrant. I doubt that he cares if we look in the truck so long as he doesn't get jammed up."

Danny walked over to the trucker who was checking out all the police activity. When he saw Danny, he started backing up towards the truck.

"Hey, buddy, hang on there. We need to talk."

The trucker froze like deer caught in the headlights.

"I don't know what you guys are doing, but whatever it is I had nothing to do with it. I haven't been here in over two weeks--you can check my log. Up until 6 am I was home in bed, and then I drove to the terminal and picked up the truck. I have been on the road coming here ever since. But I did stop for coffee once." The trucker, for whatever reason, figured he was somehow connected to what was going on here. The fact that several people wearing FBI raid jackets were walking towards him only heightened the anxiety.

"Look, buddy, we are not after you, but we would like to know what you are hauling?"

"Why?"

"Now see that's the wrong answer for someone who has nothing to hide and wants to get out of here quickly. Someone who has nothing to hide will answer the question." Danny was hoping the simple logic would set in. "Now if you tell us what's in the tank, then we will know you have nothing to hide. On the flip side, if you stick with *why*, then we are going to place hold on your vehicle and get a state truck inspection unit down here. That could take hours. Once here, they are going to make the most of the day and go over everything in the truck. They might even search the cab and report their findings. They are very anal about log books and maintenance records. So, what do you want to do?" asked Danny.

Agent Steinmetz was impressed with Danny's persuasive conversation. To add just a touch of pressure, he turned to make sure that the trucker could see the huge FBI letters on the back of his jacket.

"Shit, man, it's just home heating oil for the greenhouses. There ain't no law against delivering home heating oil is there? Go ahead and check for yourself. But I'd rather you didn't go in the cab. There's nothing illegal in there, but there might be a few things that the Mrs. might not like hearing about."

"I hear ya brother, no cab. Just show us a sample of what you are hauling, and we are done here."

There was a small spigot under the truck that allowed a sample to be produced. Sure enough, the oil was tainted with the dye indicating this was home heating oil and not to be used for commercial vehicles.

"One more favor and you can be on your way. We need to take a look from the top down of what is in the tank just to confirm the sample."

"No problem, officer, but you might get your cloths dirty climbing up there."

"That's why we get a cleaning allowance. Let's check her out."

A quick scoop of oil was retrieved from the top of the tank. It was confirmed to be dyed home heating oil. Both samples were sealed and tagged as evidence.

"Now the down side," Danny began. "This is a crime scene, and we cannot let you make your delivery."

"I have to go back to the terminal with the full load? The boss ain't gonna like it."

"Sorry about that, but you can have your boss call me. I will take the blame for turning you around and not making

195

your delivery. That's the best I can do under the circumstances."

The trucker hesitated for a moment, reluctant to leave with so much product undelivered. His boss would hit the ceiling.

"Do I have to remind you about the truck squad? We do have the Feds here; maybe we could get ICC in here for an inspection as well."

With that the trucker turned and made for the cab of the truck. "You officers ya all have a nice day. Good talkin to you."

Danny and Boom shared a knowing smile and went back to watch the lock being cut. It made a loud thud as it hit the concrete step.

Chapter 40

Danny was eager to get inside the brick structure, but Agent Steinmetz wasn't taking any chances. Even though the lock was off, he was not about to let people go charging in.

"If whoever is running this show had a guy sitting on this place with shoot to kill orders if a cop showed up, I am not taking any chances going in there. We have all the time in the world," Agent Steinmetz said. "That building isn't going anywhere. Besides, you're on overtime. Let's not kill the golden goose."

"Fine, but if we go much slower, I am going to fall asleep. So, if you find anything important make sure I am awake."

"If you want, there is a big seat in the crime scene van you can rack out on."

"You know if I do, you will find something earth shattering, and I will miss it. Not on your life--I am staying right here. "I would be careful," said Danny. Old man Worthington liked things that went boom. I would move very slowly on getting past this door."

"You think it's an IED?" asked Steinmetz.

"I wouldn't put anything past him."

"Smitty," said Agent Steinmetz. "Get the explosive ordnance guys out here."

"Aye, aye, Sir."

Then everyone grabbed a coffee and waited. The building wasn't going anywhere.

The welder cleared out his cutting gear, and two FBI bomb technicians moved in with a huge drill. They were suited up head to toe in protective bomb suits. Danny remembered the EOD guys back in the sandbox wearing the same gear. One day he got curious and asked one of the EOD guys how effective the suits were against IEDs. Danny recalled him saying; "If it's small like a hand grenade, we would be pretty safe most of the time. Distance from the blast helps. But if we are bent over the damn thing and it's a 105 round or bigger, the suit just keeps all the parts inside so it's easier to recover the entire body." Danny watched as the two bomb techs did their work. At this point he wasn't tired anymore. The whine of the drill was constant for several minutes. Like the welder with the cutting torch, water was being played over the drill bit to keep the heat down and eliminate any chance for a spark. Off to the side, a fire truck stood by at a safe distance just in case. Danny was lost in his own thoughts back in Iraq. If they had run into the same situation back there, it would have been a block of C-4 and goodbye door. But this was downtown Maidstone in the Common Wealth of Massachusetts and such things were unheard of--especially if your work sets off thirty thousand gallons of fuel oil with your little blast of the plastic explosive,C-4. Danny was brought back to the present when he heard the drill stop. The bomb techs put down the drill and inserted a thin black cable into the building. As one tech monitored a video screen, the other twisted the cable around. Silence took over the compound. From time to time the tech with the monitor would nudge the other tech, and they would both view the screen. It seemed like they were moving in slow motion. Everyone was waiting for the all clear so they could move in and have a look for themselves. Finally, the bomb tech with the monitor tapped his partner on the shoulder and gave him a thumbs up. The other tech nodded in what appeared to be agreement. The monitor was handed over to the second tech who had taken his protective helmet off. The tech continued to scan the inside of the room as the other bomb tech made his way back to Agent Steinmetz.

"The door is clear," he said. "There are no signs of wires or any attachments to the door. We can't see anything aimed at the door. Having said that, the inside of that place is just jammed packed with stuff. There are pipes, tanks, control panels, and lots of wiring. There isn't much room to move around, and I can't say I have ever seen anything like this. We did an air test, and it came back for normal levels of oxygen and high levels of petroleum-based products but not at an explosive level. I still wouldn't go in there with any open flame or anything that could create a spark. We could only get a sample from just inside door. The readings could be much higher and more dangerous in other parts of the building."

"So, what do you want to do?" asked Agent Steinmetz.

"First off we get everyone back a good distance just in case I am wrong and the place blows. We will have the fire truck with its water canon put a heavy mist on the place as a precaution. Then with a rope we pull the door open and keep our fingers crossed. If that all goes well, we enter and make a visual check. The cameras don't see everything in the detail we need. Absent any loud noises, I think we should be good to go."

"Let's do it," said Agent Steinmetz.

Neither Boom Steinmetz nor Danny liked being a spectator, but they had no choice. It was a good safe plan; and as luck would have it, nothing happened. The lead bomb tech made his way back to Agent Steinmetz and Danny while he stripped off his bomb suit. His entire body was soaked in sweat from head to toe. Bottles of water were waiting for him.

"Are you all right?" asked Danny. "You look like shit."

"Thank you for your deep concern and accurate assessment. This is the standard result of being a bomb tech. Half of the sweat is from being in that suit. The other half is from walking into a building like that, where every damn thing you look at gives the appearance it could be a bomb. What doesn't look like a bomb looks like something that could hide a bomb. There is hardly enough room to move around in there. Whatever this place is, everything inside looks brand new. It kind of reminds me of a large still but with more parts. Everything looks professionally done. There's no duct tape or jury-rigged parts. Everything is shinny and clean. Nothing has leaked or spilled on the floor. But the bottom line is I have no clue what it does. There are signs indicating flow in and flow out. There are all kinds of valves and gauges, but what they do is anyone's guess. One more thing--we are being watched."

Agent Steinmetz and Danny whirled around looking behind them. All they saw were the fireman and the other officers.

"Not out here," the bomb tech said. "Inside the brick house there are like six security cameras covering the inside. They have those amber domes over them, but you can hear the hum as they are being panned."

"Well, they had cameras on the outside. It stands to reason they would have them inside, too," said Agent Steinmetz. "We already cut the phone line so they must be on a cell phone connection. Let's take the monitor back to the crime scene van, and you can explain what you found in there."

In the van the video was gone over several times. From time to time the frames were frozen to get a prolonged look at the recording. It was all very interesting but without any real answers. That was until one of the agents processing the scene came into the van.

"I think we have something," he announced. "Here is the vial of diesel we took from the tanker truck. We have two vials from tanks one and two. That have the same color dye as that tanker did. Now here is vial four with no color to it at all. Vial four is from tank three. We checked the piping, and tanks one and two have arrows on them indicating their direction of flow is to the brick building. Tank three..."

"Tank three shows flow from the building," Agent Steinmetz stated.

"Badda Bing," said the agent. "Now I know why you are making the big bucks."

"You guys don't call me the Wiz for nothing."

The agent choked. "Sorry, boss," and beat feet out of there as fast as he could.

"Let's up load all the video and email it down to Quantico and the forensic unit and see what they think. Instead of a money laundering operation, we have a fuel laundry scam going on. But how the hell do you launder fuel oil?" Agent Steinmetz asked.

Chapter 41

The video was uploaded and sent down to the forensic guys in Quantico, Virginia. They carefully reviewed the video and sent back numerous questions. After a detailed review and numerous meetings with various experts in their respective fields, they were in complete agreement. They had no idea what it was or how it worked.

"Well, what do you suggest?" asked Agent Steinmetz of the person who was dumb enough to get tricked into making the call back to Maidstone.

"What we are looking at is something very unique. Based on what appears to be going in and what is coming out, we agree with you that this system is stripping the dye out. But no one down here has ever heard of or seen a process like that one. If it's okay with everyone up there, we want to farm this out to the petroleum industry and maybe a few of the poly tech schools. They may have a better insight on this type of thing."

"Contact whomever you want. We need to know what this does and be able to explain it, or we don't have part of the case. We have an attempted murder of a police officer. We have a conspiracy for that murder, but we believe that this is the center of the case. It won't fall apart, but explaining this as the motive would be a big help." Agent Steinmetz hung up and looked around. "Danny, go home and get some sleep. There's nothing more for you to do here."

"If you don't need me, I am going to head down to the hospital and check on Gary. The poor bastard was just taking a leak and came close to taking a twelve-gauge pellet through the brain meant for me. Then he thinks me telling him to get out is a big joke and ends up taunting the asshole who was sneaking up on him. Gary figures it's me. The asshole thinks he's been spotted and opens up. It can't get more messed up than that."

"Go ahead and see Gary, but get at least a few hours rack time. We have a lot more to do. I have to touch base with Deverse to see how he made out with the recordings and his sit down with the chief. From there we will work on a search warrant and an arrest warrant for Quenton Worthington. We know what went on here; we just don't know how. Adding that to both warrants will make an easier sell to get them signed. We are probably fine right now, but why chance it. Quenton isn't going anywhere. If he does, we have his passport flagged. He won't make it past the border."

"How much money do you think we are talking here?"

"Hard to tell at this point. The operation could have been going on for months or years. Quenton still had to buy regular diesel truck fuel the whole time. He couldn't just stop buying that fuel. It would have jumped out in a tax review. But if he played it smart and eased it in over time, Quenton could have gone unnoticed."

"What about greenhouses that aren't functioning but still using thousands of gallons of fuel?"

"No one is coming down to inspect the place. If you pay for the fuel and you pay the tax that goes along with it, no one is going to ask any questions. As long as you pay what the government expects, there won't be any red flags. The search warrant should tell us a lot. The IRS will be in on this, too, so we will be looking at all the books. The information is out there somewhere, and we will find it. Up to this point, they have been very lucky but also very good at what they were doing. This isn't some fly-by-night operation. Just look at what they put together in the brick building. Most fuel oil scams don't include stripping out the dye. They just put the home heating oil in trucks and dodge the highway inspections. That's easy enough to do if you are operating locally and not up on the highway where the D.O.T. Inspection Stations operate. Even it's a small operation, you can still make good money. The mob did it down in The Big Apple, and they were very successful. The way they stayed ahead of things was to open up a business and run the scam for a while. Even before they felt the heat, they would shut the business down, move to a new location, and open up under another name. The mob would stay one step ahead of a slow-moving bureaucracy that couldn't catch up. By the time they were nailed, the business would be closed. Everything was under assumed names so nothing could be traced.

"Now this is something entirely different. Quenton's people intended to stay in business for a long period of time. The mob never wasted time or money stripping the dye out. They just sold at a discount."

"Once I started watching greenhouse activity, I would see a tanker headed this way a couple of times a week," said Danny. "They could have been getting thirty to forty thousand gallons of fuel every week. That adds up fast if you can keep up the sales. Seeing that they could only have thirty thousand gallons of fuel on hand if they kept getting deliveries, they must have been moving it as fast as it came in."

After some thought Danny went on. "Why go to all this trouble and expense? The trucking business has always been a money maker. It isn't like the family needed more money. I can't think of a thing these people don't have. There are houses all over the country and a couple outside the U. S., what more could they want? At age twenty-five or twenty-six, Brad and Penny had a house that most forty-year-olds couldn't afford."

"How about plain old greed?" said Agent Steinmetz. "Sometimes that is what it boils down. Not a real necessity, just greed. Or maybe this was Quenton's way of getting over on the tax man. Quenton had to sink a lot of money into this venture just to get it started. He could have just used the dyed fuel for his trucks on just local runs and dodged all the state inspectors and made a sizeable return. But he wanted it all, his own personal trophy. You know like, *see how smart I am*. Greed, ego, and, of course, there is the money. The search warrant should tell us, and maybe he will too. Bragging how smart he is."

"He and Brad are both into showing off and trophy collecting," said Danny. "The cars, trucks, boats, vacation homes--they are all there. The critters Quenton has shot and the fish that he caught are all mounted on the walls of the office. Brad has some catching up to do. His car collection doesn't even come close to Quenton's, and he only has one huge house not the real estate empire that Quenton does. But Brad is just getting started."

"Sounds like we have some serious egos at play here."

"For sure," said Danny, and he headed down to Great Barrington for the hospital.

Chapter 42

At the hospital Gary was between elated and pissed. He couldn't make up his mind from one second to the next.

"Why didn't you tell me that place was hot? How come all the secrets? What the hell gives?"

"I am sorry you got shot," said Danny. "I didn't know they had an armed guard on the place. I couldn't say anything because the FBI told me not to discuss it with anyone. As soon as I knew you were in danger, I tried to get you outta there."

"How was I to know you had a camera on me? I figured you were up in the woods dug in for the night and decided to have some fun when I pulled in to take a leak. Here I am passing a few cups of coffee in a spot where I think I am completely alone, and I have the whole world watching me water the grass. Now my head is killing me, and they won't give me anything for the pain because they are worried I have a concussion. The nurse is cute, but with this pain I can't think of anything to say."

"I am sure if you ask, she might give you her phone number for future reference; but I would be careful, she does have a wedding ring."

"What ring? I didn't see a wedding ring on her left hand."

"It's not on her hand. Nurses don't have rings on duty. They get in the way of the gloves and can hold germs. She has it on a chain around her neck."

"I didn't see any chain around her neck when she came in. How do you know she has a chain around her neck?"

"Same way I knew a guy was sneaking up on you with a shotgun."

"Bullshit."

"Semi bullshit. The last time I was in here after almost getting hit by a shotgun blast like you, she was one of the nurses on duty. I was trying to make the best out of a bad situation, and I thought she was being friendly. That is until I asked her when she got off duty. That's when the necklace and the rings came out. I got them waved in my face, and the diamond appeared to be quite large."

"Smooth move for a pro like you. Did you forget about someone named Geri who has a gun?"

"I will chalk it up to the bang on my head, temporary insanity. About the time I am getting the rings flashed in my face, Geri is cranking off three rounds taking out the hitmen who were sent to kill her. Just one more quiet night in the lovely Berkshire Hills of downtown Maidstone. Nothing ever happens in Maidstone, you know that. "

"You owe me big time, pal."

"Yes, I do, but I have no idea how to make it up to you."

"I will think of something."

With that, the nurse returned to check on Gary. She gave Danny the double once over.

"Don't I know you from somewhere?" she asked.

"I don't think so, but I have brought a number of people in over the years. You might have seen me on one of those trips."

"No, I don't think so. You look so familiar. Wait a minute. You're the guy who almost got shot a while back. You came in here with a concussion to be checked out. I thought you were in some serious pain, but you still took the time to hit on me.

That was sweet. Now this guy here has a bit more class than you and is treating me like the professional and married mother of two that I am."

"Yes, Gary is a real gentleman. I have to get going, Gar. I will check on you tomorrow." Out the door Danny went a slight giggle to himself. Well, he couldn't save Gary from a shotgun blast, but he did save him from putting his foot in his mouth. I am already making it up to you, buddy, Danny thought, and he headed for the barn.

Chapter 43

As Danny pulled into the driveway, his first thought was a beer and then bed. Then the, *oh shit* happened. *I forgot about Bear, and I am way over due by hours.* Bear was going nuts when Danny arrived. He bolted out and ran Danny down when the door opened. The big smiling Labrador wasn't smiling this morning. As he cleared the door, he was leaking all over the place. Twenty yards later he was spinning around like a top trying to get in position for his next move. *Now I owe Gary and Bear. How many more people can I let down in one day?* Bear finished his business and waddled back to the barn. He seemed a little unsteady on his feet as he approached Danny holding the door open. He was pretty sure that Bear was giving him the dirtiest of looks as he walked past. Once inside he made a fast trot to the refrigerator and sat down not more than a foot from the refrigerator door. As Danny made his way inside, Bear would look at the door and then back at Danny. He repeated this several times.

"I got it, buddy, I'm sorry. Things got out of hand, and I got delayed."

Bear was not interested in excuses and repeated his alternating gaze willing Danny to open the door and feed him. The guilt trip was working. Danny opened the door; and instead of the dog food, he grabbed a chicken breast from the night before. Danny peeled off chunks of white meat. For

Bear's part, slobber was making a series of puddles on the kitchen floor. Danny gave him one bite after the other and in between managed to grab a Sam Adams for himself. The two made their way to the living area. Bear was not about to let that chicken get out of his sight. It had been a long night for both of them. Danny sipped his beer feeding Bear one small piece at a time. Knowing how hungry Bear must have been, Danny paced him so that he didn't wolf it all down at once. It could come back up as fast as it went in. Now the beer was something else. That lasted about four gulps and was gone. Danny made his way back to the refrigerator with Bear close to his side. They made the return trip, and Danny sat down in the leather recliner that had been a hand-me-down from the main house. It felt better than any bed he had ever slept in. The chicken was gone, but Bear didn't believe him. Danny held the beer between his knees and showed Bear his hands like a black jack dealer leaving the table. Bear closely examined both hands to be sure. Several licks removed any remaining chicken from Danny's hands. It was only after Bear was absolutely sure there was no more chicken that he gave up. With heavy thump he dropped onto the carpet and curdled up in a big yellow ball of fur. Danny grabbed his poncho liner and covered himself up. After a few more sips Danny drifted off. The adrenalin had worn off and the long hours and tension had consumed him. The beer just sped things up a notch.

It was hours before either one stirred. It would have been longer, but the phone kept ringing. The answering machine kicked on after six rings, but whoever was calling wasn't taking *no* for an answer. After each set of six rings, the person would hang up and call again. Danny heard only one set of bells ringing. The person on the other end was getting more and more aggravated with each attempt that wasn't answered.

Danny picked up the phone and promptly dropped it. After retrieving the phone, he gave a very weak hello.

The caller was not pleased. "This is Captain Malloy of the Massachusetts State Police."

Danny's eyes popped wide open, and he was instantly awake. "Is Geri okay?"

"I am not calling about Geri. I am the acting Chief of Police for Maidstone, and you still have a cruiser out and are not on duty. I want that vehicle returned immediately."

"So, Geri is okay?"

"I have no idea how Geri is and, frankly, don't care. I am in charge for now, and I want that vehicle back or you're suspended." Click.

Danny looked outside, and sure enough there was the marked unit in the driveway. How the hell could I forget to bring back the cruiser? But then again, the captain had to know what was going on. He could have sent two guys with the extra keys to pick it up. Danny let Bear out to do his thing and then made his way to the cruiser. He was still in uniform from the night before. It was less than pristine, and even the U. S. Marshall raid jacket was rumpled from being slept in. After arriving at the control center, Danny walked in and hung up the keys on the rack.

"Put me in the book for a personal day tonight," he told the dispatcher.

"Got it but Captain Malloy wants to see you."

Danny mumbled something and walked down the hallway to the chief's office. A soft knock was followed by a sharp *enter*.

"You wanted to see me, chief?" Danny was standing tall in front of the desk. He expected to be asked about the events of the night before. That was not what he got.

"Is that how you people report to the commanding officer of your department?" Captain Malloy demanded.

Danny wasn't sure what to say. He hadn't been talked to like that since boot camp. "Sorry, Sir, I am a little out of it. It was a long night, and I just woke up."

"Sorry won't cut it, Mister. Look at you--you're a mess. What are you doing in a U. S. Marshall's raid jacket? Take that thing off right now."

Danny was trying to figure out what nightmare he had just walked into. Was he still asleep? Didn't this guy know about the shooting and the investigation? He must, he is here as the acting chief. He took the jacket off as ordered folding it over his arm.

Captain Malloy slowly rose from the chair glaring at him. Danny for his part could not for the life of him figure out what was going on.

"So, cowboy, you got the new chief fired. Feeling pretty cocky, are you? All dressed up in a federal raid jacket. Well, let me tell you something. You pull any shit with me and you won't have to worry about getting fired. Cornell is a friend of mine from back in the old days when you college boys would never get on the force. All pretty boy and book smart but with no balls. You're going to work for me, and you are going to do it my way. I suggest to you is that you go out on medical leave to straighten yourself out. You have been through a lot for a pretty boy, and god knows you can't handle it with all your drinking and pill popping. Then you can just disappear into the sunset, and we can all forget you. I will make sure you are gone just like I got that princess of a state trooper of yours sent as far away as possible. You have screwed with the last real police officer. Now get the hell out of my office, I can't stand the smell."

Danny made no move for the door. When Captain Malloy looked up, he was still there. The look of anger was set in the captain's jaw. His face turned beet red, and the veins pulsed on his forehead.

"I told you to get the fuck out and you better start moving, or I will suspend you for insubordination."

Still Danny made no move towards the door. The chief snatched up his phone and barked into it. "Get me a ranking officer in here right now. I want this insubordinate piece of crap removed from my office now."

Still Danny made no move.

The detective lieutenant arrived at the door. "You wanted to see me?"

"Get this piece of crap out of here."

The detective lieutenant looked at the captain then at Danny. Finally, he looked around the room to see who the chief was talking about. "You mean Danny?"

"Yes. Now!"

The lieutenant looked at Danny and then at the chief. Danny and the lieutenant made eye contact. "Hey, lieutenant, long time no see."

The detective lieutenant was almost as tired and used up as Danny and wasn't ready for any games. He was trying to figure out what was going on when Danny pulled the raid jacket back on.

"I told you to take that fucking thing off."

"No, chief, you see……" and Danny pulled out his federal ID and badge and held it up for the chief to see. "I am a U. S. Marshall and a Maidstone police officer. Now that the detective lieutenant is here, I think maybe I should read you your rights."

"Read ME my rights, you snot nosed kid. I was reading people their rights before you were born. Go fuck yourself."

"Have it your way," said Danny. "But you are going to be arrested for threatening a federal officer and abuse of your position as acting chief of police."

"Lieutenant, get him out of here before I kick the shit of this college boy punk."

"Captain," said Lieutenant Nanfito, "he is a U. S. Marshall. I was there when the U. S. Attorney personally handed him his federal credentials."

The captain was taken aback but not much. "Federal or not, I still want his sorry ass out of here and banished from this building."

Danny looked at the captain not sure what to think. It was too late for the captain anyway. He had made his own bed, and now he had to sleep in it.

"Just to let you know, everything you said, every word, every threat has been recorded pursuant to a federal wiretap warrant."

"Bullshit." But the captain wasn't looking or feeling as confident as he was a few minutes ago.

"If you brought anything with you, I suggest you get it all together, so you don't have to rush around later," said Danny. "Hey, lieutenant, let's get a coffee, and you can fill me in on what happened after I left the scene."

The two Maidstone officers left the chief's office. Nanfito didn't take his eyes off the captain as they moved out of the room. He wasn't sure if he would try something, but he wasn't about to turn his back on him. The few words that Nanfito heard would be enough to get him removed as acting chief of police at Maidstone. His job as a state police captain would certainly be in jeopardy. It might be a good time for the captain to put in his retirement papers. The events of the past few hours had Detective Lieutenant Dominic Nanfito wondering what was going to happen next and what else

214

didn't he know. Maybe Danny could fill him in. The idea of another cup of coffee took his acid filled belly to a new level. No more coffee, I have to eat something.

Chapter 44

Detective Lieutenant Dominic Nanfito had been a Maidstone police officer for over fifteen years. He had stayed off the radar not making waves and going with the flow. He had no connections, but at the same time he had never pissed anyone off. When the promotion process for detective lieutenant began, he wasn't the chief's pick. Chief Cornell had his own officer in mind, but there was a hitch. His pick had scored a whapping sixty-nine on the promotional exam. The oral board was better with an eighty. But that was only because two of the five board members were in the bag for the chief. Their padded scores on the oral board brought the chief's pick up, but not high enough to make a difference in the final ranking. The three low scoring board members at first could not figure out how their almost matching scores were so much different than the high scoring other two. When the two high scorers gave their reasoning, it made sense that they had been coached by someone as to who should be the next detective lieutenant.

Nanfito managed to score an eighty-nine on the written and an eighty-six on the oral. With the chief's pick so far behind number one, it would have never gotten past the police commission. With extreme reluctance Sergeant Dominic Nanfito was promoted to Detective Lieutenant. In keeping with his low-profile policy, Nanfito knew he would be under the microscope of the chief. It was always *Yes, sir, chief. I'm on it, chief. Whatever you need, chief, I can help.* After a time, the chief seemed to get used to the outcome, and Nanfito was left alone. No waves, no problems, and absolutely no complaints. He wasn't the chief's boy, but he was not about to screw up a good thing. Terminal midnights on the road sucked big time. Nanfito had had enough checking businesses and dodging skunks and raccoons breaking into dumpster and garbage cans. The late-night foraging by wild animals resulted in frantic calls from the city folk, reporting a home invasion in progress. Now it was day shift, Monday through Friday, with weekends off like a normal person. His wife was ecstatic. He had time for all the kids' sports activities. If he did get called out, it was for something of importance, not felonious skunks running amuck in the neighborhood. Even then, call outs were rare. Department policy did not allow overtime. If it were construction or extra duty traffic jobs, then that was okay. Those costs were billed to whomever they were working for. The town actually made money on the road jobs, tacking on a processing fee to each hour. Part of the chief's bonus came from how much overtime was returned to the town at the end of the budget. This old-school Yankee town being fiscally frugal had its rewards if only for the chief's benefit. Nanfito didn't like it, but he knew the rules, and he knew he couldn't change them. He wasn't a Detective Lieutenant Snyder who could be bought, but he wasn't about to screw up a good thing when he had it made.

"When did Malloy get here?" Danny asked.

"When you were down at the hospital, the FBI walked Chief Cornell out. The commissioner for the state police was here with a number of his staff, and he left Captain Malloy as acting chief. Malloy as you know was the western district patrol supervisor for the state police and the commish decided that he knew the area the best and left him here in temporary command pending a replacement by the town police commission. I would say his first day didn't go so well. How is Gary doing?"

"Grazing shot to his head with no penetration. He has a serious headache and mild concussion but should be out today or tomorrow at the latest. The only thing that saved him is the mutt fired the sawed off from so far away that the buck shot had spread in a huge pattern. He jumped the gun when Gary yelled at him thinking it was me and spooked him. He thought he had been spotted and opened up. Gary for his part cranked off a shitload of rounds. When the mutt fired the second time, one pellet caught Gary. He thought he was dead, so he figured he would get the shooter before he checked out. Gary concentrated on the muzzle blast he saw and slowly fired off several rounds and with a much better aim. One of his rounds caught the guy in the leg. As they say, the rest is history."

"Why is Malloy so pissed?"

"He blames me for getting Chief Cornell fired."

"I couldn't help but hear him yelling about you being a drunken pill popper; what's that all about?"

"Chief Cornell was telling all his old school contacts that I had a drug and alcohol problem. Remember the stag we all went to?"

"Sure, you made an early exit."

"Oh, yes, and I had a Great Barrington captain waiting for me on the way home. How many captains do you think go on the road looking for drunks? Off duty, mind you."

"No way!"

"Luckily someone was looking out for me because that night I didn't even have one beer. He gave me the field breath test, and it came back zero point zero zero eight. After we chatted for a while, he let me go. I heard that the captain got on Cornell's case and read him the riot act. It seems he wasn't the only one Cornell called."

"Maybe you should take a few days off."

"I have way too much to do, but most of it will be report writing. Like as in forever writing."

"I hear ya."

They made their way to Nanfito's office. Danny sipped his coffee and Nanfito munched on a few Rolaids. The conversation was light, and they were winding down and starting to drift off when they were startled by the dispatcher on the PA. "Gilcrest to the control center on the double."

Shit, what now, Danny thought.

The dispatcher looked at Danny in a strange way. It was a look of bewilderment and confusion--a look of surprise, a questioning look. It's an Inspector from the U. S. Attorney's office MS Sheriden wants to speak to you."

"Lieutenant, can we take this in your office?"

"Of course."

"You were expecting a call from the U. S. Attorney?" the dispatcher asked. "No, but I better take it."

Danny and the lieutenant moved back down the hall to Nanfito's office. Danny entered as the phone was ringing. The door was closed, so Danny would have some privacy. LT Nanfito had no intention of entering the office and listening in on the conversation.

"This is your office, please come in."

"Are you sure?"

"Absolutely!"

Ms. Sheriden was surprised by the strange and getting stranger turn of events. Danny filled her in and explained the long-time connections between Chief Cornell and his old school police buddies. For his part Detective Lieutenant

Nanfito was only getting half of the conversation. Most of the talking was being done by Ms. Sheriden.

"Danny," asked the U. S. Attorney, "because we have issues with the state police, who should we appoint as acting chief?"

"You're asking me?"

"Yes."

Danny started thinking, reviewing everyone in the department with any time on the job. It was a short list. Many names didn't last more than a nanosecond. "Hey, lieutenant, you have any vacation or holiday time scheduled for the next few weeks?"

"No, but even if I did, there is no way I can take time off with this mess in front of me."

"You do have Timmy O'Rourke as your detective sergeant. He has his shit together."

"Yes, but this is my case."

"We shall see," said Danny. "Ms. Sheriden, the name that jumps out at me is Detective Lieutenant Dominic Nanfito from our P.D. in Maidstone."

"Excellent! I want to see him in my office. Could you have him call me?"

"Hold on, he is right here." Danny handed the phone to one dog tired and confused Detective Lieutenant.

The conversation was brief and one sided. With a final *Yes, Ma'am* the LT handed the phone back to Danny.

"Keep in mind that for the time being you **are** a U. S. Marshall, and you take orders from me. Is that understood?"

"Yes, ma'am," and the line went dead.

"What the hell did you just volunteer me for?"

"I would suggest you bring Timmy in ASAP and make sure he is up to speed on the investigation. You are going to otherwise be occupied for the near future."

Chapter 45

Danny spent most of the next few days dictating and editing his report, reliving every moment with each key stroke.

Detective Lieutenant Dominic Nanfito knew he should be pissed at Danny but at the same time had this notion he could be trusted. Either way he had so much to do that he was far too busy to sit and think. He had to reorganize the police department. There were now two fulltime officers who were pulled from duty. Danny was out on his U. S. Marshall assignment and Gary out on medical leave. The biggest case the department had ever had, and he wasn't going to be the lead detective. Still, he was now the acting chief and could do pretty much what he wanted.

The FBI had the scene and numerous agents teamed up with Maidstone officers watching locations that were about to be raided. No one was leaving anything to chance. With such high-profile suspects as a chief of police and a multi-millionaire with connections and family throughout western Massachusetts, no one was about to sign a warrant without absolutely ironclad probable cause. It was going to be a higher standard, proof beyond a reasonable doubt. Taking on a chief meant taking on all chiefs. When one chief was threatened, they all felt threatened. If the justice department could take out one of them, then everyone else was vulnerable. Now no one was untouchable in a little fiefdom when something like this happens. If the case against Cornell was tight, the other chiefs would step back and let the chips fall where they may, not wanting to draw too much attention to their departments and to create as much distance as possible.

Danny got an email from Geri that she was being recalled to the states. She had a couple of weeks to wrap up what she was doing and would soon be home.

The hitman had made the connection between Anthony Carl and Quenton. Now Worthington, for his part, incriminated himself when he called Chief Cornell to fix things after the hitman tried to take out the wrong guy. That would be more than enough for conspiracy to commit murder. Of course, given enough time and several high-priced lawyers, that statement could be made to sound like a good citizen was asking the chief to do his job. As in, *Hey, this is a real problem, and we're counting on you to take care of it and bring the suspects to justice*. For Danny there was only one question left: will they find the evidence that Quenton paid off Detective Lieutenant Snyder to bag the case of Penny Worthington's murder.

The phone rang bringing Danny back to reality.

"You have some time?" asked Deverse.

"I now work for the U. S. Attorney. If she says I have time, then of course I have time."

"Smart-ass. I will see you at the barn in an hour. Bring beer."

Beer, Danny thought. I could really use a beer, but I will be asleep before I finish it. Danny collected everything and made his way to the chief's office to checkout with Acting Chief Nanfito. Danny saw that the door was closed and locked, so he lightly knocked on the door. There was no response. The secretary offered, "He isn't in there."

"Did he go to the crime scene?" Danny asked.

"No, he is in his office."

Now Danny was confused. How if he is in his office if he wasn't in his office? The secretary saw the puzzled look. "When I said he wasn't in there, I meant that he wasn't in the chief's office. He is in his own office in the bureau. He told me he wasn't going in there for anything. Bad karma or something like that."

Danny nodded and made his way to the bureau where he found one very busy police officer. Nanfito saw Danny and shaking his head gave him a dirty look.

"What did I ever do to you to deserve this?" Nanfito wanted to know.

"You were the only guy with rank in this department who seemed to want to do police work, and you weren't interested in the side perks."

Nanfito almost managed a smile.

"I am heading to the barn to meet with Agent Deverse, want to come along?"

"I would love to, but I have my hands full right here."

"I had a Captain in the Marines who tried to do everything. Needless to say, it didn't work, and things were a mess, especially when we were deployed. When we hit the sandbox, it wasn't an eight- or twelve-hour day. It was twenty-four hours nonstop, and no one can go very long without some decent sleep. The first sergeant let him run for a couple of days until he was good and burned out. About that time the rest of us were about to kill him. Top sat him down and explained delegation and coordination. No one would think less of him, if he didn't do everything, and no one expected him to. Call in the supervisors and let them supervise. You be the coordinator. Step back and watch. Everything isn't going to be done exactly as you might

223

envision, but the point is things will get done. Have the supervisors take responsibility for their units and buy into the success or failure. You don't have to do it all yourself."

All Danny got was a very tired nod. But it was enough.

When Danny hit the package store, the clerk seemed surprised to see him.

"You're still here?" was all the clerk could say.

"And where am I supposed to be?" Danny asked.

The clerk could not come up with anything to say and rang up the sale. Danny took the two six packs of Sam Adams and made for the door. He called out over his shoulder, "I will be back, maybe not tomorrow, but soon. I am not going anywhere." All Danny could think of was what must the town be thinking now of this quaint location in the Berkshire Hills.

Deverse was waiting for him at the barn. Bear made a break for the outside and gave Agent Deverse a cursory sniff as he went by.

"That can't be the same dog that chomped the mob guy who broke in here?"

"That, sir, is in fact Bear, the attack dog. Bear has never been aggressive before or after the break in. Somehow, Bear knew that what was going down was wrong and went after the mob guy like a Pitbull. Don't ask me how he knew. I keep asking him, but he won't give it up. I have even bribed him with cookies, and all he does is stare at me and wait me out."

They waited for Bear to take care of business and re-enter the barn. It was spacious and comfortable. They each took a seat in the mission style recliners and opened a beer. Bear made his way to the right side of Agent Deverse's chair and parked himself there.

"You should scratch his head--he likes it, and it will relax you. If you wait too long, you're going to get your hand bumped and that will have beer going all over the place." As if on cue, Bear's nose went under Deverse's hand and up went the beer. Fortunately, after being warned, Agent Deverse had a firm grip on the bottle and only a little spilled. Deverse shifted the beer to his left hand and dutifully began stroking Bear's fat head.

"I don't know if I can drink beer, pay attention to Bear, and fill you in."

"You're an FBI agent, you can do anything. Give it a shot."

"Okay, once upon a time......."

Chapter 46

"We managed to find out what was going on with the brick building," Deverse continued. "Quantico came up with a chemical engineer who is a professor at MIT. To say the guy is brilliant is an understatement. We took him out to the greenhouses and had him take a look. For about an hour he walked through the cramped quarters. He kept grunting and nodding. He would talk to himself and make notes on a pad. One time, I was able to look over his shoulder and see his notes. I couldn't make out one word he had written. There were also a bunch of math equations. Finally, he stands in the middle of the building, turns, and makes a profound statement, the first statement I could understand."

"And that was?"

"WOW!"

"That's it, *WOW*? That's our expert witness's take on the brick house?"

"Oh no, that was just the only part of his statement I really understood. From there he goes on to explain the process from the dyed diesel coming in and the clear diesel coming out. It would take another Ph.D. to understand what this guy said. I told him that at some point he may have to explain as to how this operation functioned to a judge and jury who don't have his extensive background. He gave me a very frustrated shrug like, *everyone should be able understand this process because I just explained it to you.* But he gave it a shot. The dye, he said, really doesn't mix with the fuel the way most people think. The molecules of dye are suspended in the molecules of diesel. They don't combine. Just like gasoline and ethanol don't mix. If you left gasoline mixed with ethanol sit long enough, the two will separate with the lighter ethanol rising to the top. You would be able to see the separation. What you wouldn't see is the ethanol that was still suspended in the gasoline. That is where the diesel and the dye are different. There is only a small amount of dye in the diesel to give it the distinctive color. If a lot were put in, that would affect the burning properties of the fuel. What keeps the fuel dyed and not separating is the motion of pumping; and when it is in the trucks, the movement of the trucks does the same thing. That is one of the reasons why the mixture of ethanol and gasoline is bad for seasonal equipment. The longer it sits, the more the two separate."

"So, what does the equipment in the brick house do?"

"As the dyed fuel enters the building, it is electrically charged. Each molecule accepts the charge at a different level. As the fuel passes through the pipes, the dye is drawn off, but not all of it because there is still a fuzzy layer where there is fuel and dye. However, the color is greatly reduced. Then they add a bleaching agent which further reduces the color of the dye. It doesn't eliminate it completely, but to the naked eye of a truck inspector it would appear to be clear. Now if you put it under a microscope or did a gas chromatography with a MA-spectrum test, the dye would show up. No one does those tests. The end result is what appears to be legal fuel for vehicles but with no state or federal road taxes being paid."

"So, this means Quenton is saving money on each and every gallon?"

"For sure! He is using it in his own trucks, and it appears that he is selling the fuel wholesale to other companies. He isn't making as much per gallon as the fuel that he uses, but it is all a positive cash flow. The fuel that is coming into the greenhouses is being used as a tax-deductible business expense. This is all part of the overhead for running the greenhouse business."

"How much did he make?"

"Until we hit the place with a search warrant and get all his records, it is only a guess. We have no idea how long he has been doing this bleaching. We don't know how much fuel he has laundered. We also don't know what he paid wholesale for the dyed fuel, and we don't know what he is selling it for. Once the forensic accountants get in there, we will nail it down. But the guess is somewhere in the hundreds of thousands maybe even in to the millions."

"How can he hide it; the place is vacant. Nothing is going on here."

"Would you believe that he does own a series of greenhouses over in New York State that are in full operation? He uses those to conceal the fuel that comes here. There are also other expenses associated with the vacant greenhouses. According to tax records, the Worthington trucking business is on the decline resulting in less fuel being used for the trucks while the fact of the matter is that he has been adding trucks every year and expanding the business. As far as the IRS goes, as long as you pay what the government thinks you owe, no one is going to go checking on all this other activity. They have enough obvious and not very bright cheats to chase after. If the operation appears legit, they never get a second look. No one comes down to Maidstone to see if there are greenhouses. Now the place in New York State uses more fuel than it could possibly justify, but there aren't any solid projections of what a greenhouse should use for heat to measure that something questionable wrong. Quenton Worthington is one very smart guy and rolling in the big bucks. The fact that his trucking business is profitable all by itself without the laundered fuel just shows how greedy this guy is."

"What about Chief Cornell; how does he figure into this?" Danny wanted to know.

"After several long chats with the former chief, it appears that Quenton was grooming the chief for future use. He really didn't ask the chief for anything until the ambush at the greenhouses. By the way, how is Gary doing?"

"Mild concussion, and what's going to turn into an awesome scar. He should be out any day now and has a few weeks of medical leave coming. Says he is headed to Cape Cod for a few days to consider his future. He is a little spooked about going back on the road. I can't say that I blame him."

"You were shot at a lot more than Gary was," said Deverse, "but you keep going back on the road."

"The first time I was shot at was in Iraq. I didn't have a choice about going back on the road. I had to suck it up and head down the street following the Gunny. There was no time or opportunity to consider not going. In the Marines you don't have a choice. Conditioning. Gary never expected to get shot at. I always did. So, when do we go pickup Quenton?"

"There will be no *we* in picking up Quenton. He is already pissed at you enough to pay a hitman to sit in the woods; and if you showed up, well, we know where that goes. We have been sitting on his home and the business since this went down. So far, he hasn't been to the house and has been at the trucking company 24/7 for the last few days. No one has seen him leave, though he could have gone out in one of the trucks or other vehicles from inside the loading docks. But we have no indication that he has moved from his office. He is still taking calls in there. From the sounds of the conversations, it is business as usual. We can only listen for a few minutes, and the wire tape monitor has to disconnect if the call does not sound relevant to the case. He doesn't sound like a man getting ready to run or even concerned about the chief being arrested or the hitman situation."

"I want to at least be there when this goes down."

"We can work that out as long as no one sees you until he is cuffed and escorted out of the building. How about we let you re-cuff him with your cuffs once he comes out?"

"No, that would look like I had to let you guys do the heavy lifting while I sat it out. It will be enough to see him taken in. I don't need the arrest. I do need to make the case that he fixed the outcome of Brad's trial. That's what I need."

"With the search warrant, we should be able to make the money connection to Quenton. The trail has to be somewhere, and we will find it. Now I have to get back to Ms. Sheriden. This is like the tenth draft of the search and arrest warrants we have done, and she is still not satisfied. When we are finally done, these warrants will be used as the gold standard for training down at Quantico. I have done dozens--maybe hundreds--of warrants, and they have never been torn to shit by the U. S. Attorney like these have been."

"Are you sure she is going to approve them at some point?"

"Yes! She has already said they were fine with a big **BUT**. Ms. Sheriden keeps finding minor details that she wants corrected so down the road all the potential grounds for having the warrants thrown out and the search rendered invalid won't fly. She isn't taking any chances. Ms. Sheriden has put together two teams of attorneys. One is for the prosecution, and the other is for the defense. Each draft goes to the two teams, and they present their cases against each other. When they find an error or what could be perceived as an error, the warrant is changed. It is driving us nuts but will pay off in the long run. We know Quenton will hire the absolutely best of everything, so the work is done from that angle."

"Oh boy! This is going to drag on for years."

"In all likelihood, yes. I gotta run. Keep in touch. You still have the FBI phone so call if you need anything."

Danny had a lot to think about, and now he had the time.

Chapter 47

Danny had had enough. He decided that it was *me* time. No one was watching; and after all the hours with the case, he had no idea which ones he would get paid for. At this point, he didn't care. All he knew was that he had to put some distance between himself and Maidstone. His face and name were just a bit too well known to be hanging anywhere in close proximity to the action. The FBI and the justice department were doing their thing, and he would get enough warning to get back in time for the fireworks. Geri was still across the pond with at least a week before she could come home.

"Bear, we are outta here." All Bear knew was that there was food in the pack, and they were headed for the Jeep. In Bear's world that was more than enough. For Danny it was a good start.

They made their way to Mount Greylock and headed for the top. Greylock isn't a big mountain, but it does have a steep drop off on the western side. The views are fantastic on a clear day, and the show is breath taking. Danny found a nice flat ledge to sit and have lunch with Bear. Almost immediately, the show started. Hang gliders set up on the side of the mountain on a good size ledge, good size if you were standing there. Awfully tiny if this were your launching ramp. One after the other, gliders would take the few steps at a trot to the edge and then over they would go. The next few seconds would have each dropping like a rock close to the cliff. The wings would gain lift and forward motion, and each would silently drift off away from Danny and the mountain. A few were fortunate enough to have a slight wind coming from the west as they launched. It was almost as if they had stepped on an invisible carpet. There was almost no drop; and if the breeze were strong enough, they actually rose instead of dropping. To Danny this was all amazing. Bear, on the other hand, did not like giant flying insects anywhere near his food and barked his head off at each launch. For several hours Danny watched as people took flight. Maidstone was a million miles away at least for a short period of time. He mused that he might actually want to try hang gliding sometime. He thought about the danger of crashing into the side of the granite cliff and his chances for surviving the wreck. Then he asked himself what was more dangerous, being a police officer in Maidstone or hang gliding? *Shit!*

Bear loved hiking. Ritz crackers and cheddar cheese were aces with Bear. He could do this every day. But even Bear knew that the sound of a cell phone ring always meant that something was about to change.

"Yeah, Tom, what is it?" asked a now focused Danny.

"We got the warrants. We are going to hit the place tomorrow. I need you at the barn at 5am. Is that a problem?"

"Wouldn't miss it for the world!"

"Have you ever been inside the trucking company complex?"

"Sure, a few times. Under the old, old chief we would get dispatched there when someone was getting fired. If it were a trucker or say a dock worker, we would be there when he pulled in. One officer would stay with the guy's car along with a security officer. A second officer with two security

233

officers would escort the guy to personnel where he would be terminated and then down to clean out his locker. Now two police officers and three security officers were there when the guy was told not to come back, or he would be arrested for trespass. It worked. The big show was when Quenton fired someone from the management team. That was a real dog and pony show. Quenton let the guy get to his desk, and two security guys and a police officer would walk up to him. The personnel director would announce that Mr. Worthington wanted to see him NOW. If the guy wasn't shittin a brick before, when he saw security and the cop he was. Up to Quenton's office everyone would go, and Quenton Worthington would give his separation speech. The few people I escorted out had usually done something that involved stealing from the company. Padding expense accounts was one guy's trip out the door. I heard walking out with company property was the next most common violation. The one guy who really stands out was the one who was writing checks to a fake company he had created. Most of the checks were not that big, two hundred here, five hundred there. He kept them small so it wouldn't draw attention. Bottom line is that he still got caught. Quenton would lecture the individual about honesty, trust, loyalty, and the virtues of being a good employee. Next was an escort to his car, off the grounds, never to return. Quenton was very big on loyalty and honesty. Funny how he decided what is right and wrong."

"This time," said Agent Deverse, "Quenton will be the one getting walked out. We have the blue prints of the building, but we don't know how access works. How do we get to his office, and what areas do we need to cover in case he decides to pull a Houdini?"

"He is well insulated from direct access. Reception is on the first floor, and he is up on the fourth or fifth floor. I am not even sure how many floors there are. His office overlooks the inside loading area and has windows that overlook a small park out back. Reception is manned by a security officer who checks you in and then hands you off to one of several secretaries depending on who you are there to see. The door to get past the security officer is locked, and you have to be buzzed in. The secretaries on the inside call down to which ever department you are there to visit, and an escort comes down from that department to pick you up. That next door is also locked with the secretary permitting access. There are stairs to take you to Quenton's level, but we always used the elevator. Now there is his secretary in the outer room and waiting area who has to buzz you into Quenton's office. His office is really three rooms. There is a conference room with a table for meetings. There is a second conference room with large windows overlooking the loading area. Finally, there is his office, which is about one thousand square feet. It is a cross between an expensive hunting lodge and mahogany palace, and it is very intimidating. From his office you can make your way outside by his private staircase that goes out the back. The door is heavy duty, and it would take Godzilla on steroids to kick it down. There is a second set of stairs that goes from the windowed conference room down to the loading docks. If you were considering rushing the place, forget it. All he doors are locked, and you need to be buzzed through or have a card key."

"You say that the office is like a hunting lodge. Are there firearms in the room?"

"Wall to wall with gun cases of some of the most expensive firepower I have ever seen. Rifles, shotguns, pistols, you name it. He shoots long range competition at Camp Perry every year. He is very good, too. He thinks nothing of plunking down twenty or thirty grand for a shotgun he might only shoot in one competition before it goes on display in the office."

"Okay, so he is well armed, has great security, and there are going to be several dozen innocent bystanders who might get in the way. This isn't shaping up to be an easy takedown. I'll get back to you."

"Back to work, Bear, vacation is over." Danny took a last look out to the west. He had watched eight or ten people walk off the cliff and just float away. Some dropped dangerously close to the cliff face but recovered nicely. Others just floated off the cliff without a hitch. Danny and the FBI needed a plan just like these guys that was flexible. Danny hoped it wouldn't be some big FBI production like the one that almost got him killed.

Chapter 48

Danny had the coffee on when Agent Deverse arrived at the barn. Bear had already had breakfast and was back in bed. Bear gave Agent Deverse the briefest of looks and then went back to his nap.

"Here's how we are going to do this. We are going to lock the place down and ask him to come out and submit to the arrest. We have U. S. Marshalls securing the two secondary doors. Two teams from FBI hostage rescue will be in vans at the front and the back. They won't deploy unless this turns to shit or he barricades himself in his office. I will be taking three agents with me up to his suite. We clear out the secretary and anyone else in the area. There will be a call made to his attorney as to what is going down. We will have the attorney call Quenton and tell him to surrender."

"Then what?"

"Then we wait. As long as we can isolate him in the office, there is no reason to kick the door in. He isn't going anywhere, and there is no need to get anyone shot forcing the issue. If he doesn't surrender immediately, we start with a negotiator and wait him out."

"How long will you wait?"

"As Ms. Sheriden said and I quote, 'As long as it takes.' No one is getting killed on this operation if at all possible."

"A million things could go wrong," said Danny.

"We are going to do this as quietly as possible. Everyone going inside through the front door will be in suits looking like the regular business types. We intend to get to his outer office before he knows we are there. An agent is going to make a call to Quenton posing as the secretary for his attorney and keep him on the phone until everyone is in place. We have to move fast before any of the security or staff tips him off. Hopefully, he won't take any calls while waiting for his attorney to come on the line. Once we get to his office, the other teams will deploy to cover the doors. They will have visual on the doors the whole time. When everyone is in place, the raid jackets come out, so there is no question who we are. The calls are made to his office and the attorney and then we wait."

"Where am I while all this going down?"

"You are going to be with the HRT unit at the front doors inside the van. Once he is cuffed, I will let you know; and you can come out and see the perp walk. Unless there is some real problem, the HRT guys will not leave the van. You ready for this?"

"Good to go, but I gotta hit the head one more time. Six cups of coffee weren't a good idea if I am going to be sitting in a van for God knows how long."

"Not to worry, we always have several empty Gatorade bottles for just such situation."

"Nice touch, very thoughtful."

The group formed outside of town in the back parking lot of the Butternut Brewery. This early in the morning, the place was deserted. A few empty cars were still in the lot. Danny scanned the cars wondering which ones got lucky and which ones were too shitfaced to drive. He showed Deverse his hiding place the night the "cougar" came on to him. It wasn't much of a hiding place, now that daylight began to brighten

238

up the sky. Danny's saving grace that night was that she had assumed he was long gone, and the dappling of shadows broke up his outline. All the agents and marshals were getting their briefings, and each one had to independently give Agent Deverse a word-for-word brief back. Nothing was left to chance in the planning. Timing was of the upmost importance. If everything went accordingly, they would have agents in Quenton Worthington's office in less than two minutes from the time they hit the gate. There would be no sirens. No lights. No running. No shouting. Everything on the outside would look like the normal arrival of several executives for a business meeting.

Still, Danny had many misgivings. Why hadn't Quenton left the building for several days? Was he planning something? Why were his phone conversations so normal? He had to know that something was going on. Danny thought back to so many raids he had done as a Marine. He recalled that the ones with the most detail and practice almost always turned to shit in a heartbeat. No great plan survives first contact. The other side always has a vote as to the outcome. Overall, this was a good plan with various levels of backup just in case everything did turn to shit.

Chapter 49

Everyone was quiet, not one word had been spoken in the van since they left the brewery. The vehicles were lined up just out of sight of the main entrance guard shack. Agent Deverse's voice came over the radio. It was soft, almost a whisper; but it jolted everyone like a bolt of lightning.

"Everyone on their toes. Show time!"

The first agents pulled up to the guard shack and quickly informed the security officer that the FBI was there with a search warrant. The security officer was directed to a chair and told not to use the radio or phone. A second agent opened the gate and gave three quick clicks on the radio. The next vehicle drove through the gate to the front of the main office. Three agents exited the vehicle carrying briefcases as though they were there for a meeting. They quickly moved inside and gained access to the inner office. All the phones were quickly placed on hold and the employees directed into a conference room. There were three more clicks on the radio, and with that three more agents exited the second vehicle and made their way upstairs to Mr. Worthington's secretary. Slowly the two unmarked HRT vans moved up and drove into the complex and took up their assigned positions. No one gave them a second look. The gate was now secured. The security officer was directed to tell anyone requesting access that there had been a security breach that was being checked, and it would be a few minutes before they would be allowed in. Agent Deverse led the other two agents through the door to Mr. Worthington's secretary using a key card he had retrieved from the security officer at the front desk. A look of surprise and shock crossed her face as she reached for the phone. Her hand froze in midair as Agent Deverse held up the warrant in one hand and waved a finger at her with the other. In a soft whisper he told her, "FBI with a warrant, put the phone down."

The secretary was sucking wind in deep breaths and in slow motion returned the phone to the cradle. In a cracking voice she said, "He is expecting you."

Agent Deverse was shocked, "He knows we are here?"

"He knew you were coming, and I was to expect to you."

"So, he doesn't know we are here right now outside his office?"

"I don't think so. I had no idea that you were coming up."

Agent Deverse clicked his radio three times. Everything was going as planned and on time. Two more agents from the first floor joined Agent Deverse and his team in the secretary's area.

"Is he planning anything?" Agent Deverse asked.

"He said he was going to be arrested and to show you in when you arrived."

Agent Deverse looked around the room, and the other agents took up positions away and off to the side of the doorway.

"Here's what you're going to do, Amanda. I want you to call him. Tell him we are here with a warrant for his arrest, and we would like him to come out with his hands up."

The secretary hesitated. Agent Deverse could see the look of pain and doubt on her face.

"Look, we don't want anyone to get hurt. Not us, not you, and not Mr. Worthington. We just want a peaceful surrender. After you make the call, please head downstairs. There is an agent down there who will instruct you on where to go."

With great reluctance the secretary made the call. It was brief. She said everything Agent Deverse had requested. Quenton Worthington's response was professional.

"Thank you, Amanda. Tell them I will be out in just a moment." But that was followed by a strange request. "Please leave the office and know that none of this is your fault. Goodbye."

Amanda replaced the phone in the cradle and slowly stood up moving toward the door. Agent Deverse was trying to understand what he had just heard. He kept repeating what Quenton Worthington had said. It just seemed odd. Agent Deverse radioed all units that contact had been made and that the subject was going to surrender shortly. As he finished his transmission, a God-awful explosion came from Quenton Worthington's office. Everyone moved at once trying to find cover and stay away from the office door. Amanda was only a few steps away down the hall. When she heard the blast, she screamed in terror. It appeared to the agents on the floor that she had been hit. Amanda was laying there thrashing on the floor in agony. Her clothing was soaking through.

Agent Deverse was back on the radio. His voice was mechanical, devoid of the surprise and urgency of the quickly crumbling situation. The voice sounded more like a recording than a human being.

"We have shots fired by the suspect. One civilian is down. HRT to the main office now. Release the ambulance into the compound. The casualty is in a safe location for treatment. Secure all exits and evacuate all employees away from the building. Get the Wiz up here with a pinhole camera." Agent

Deverse didn't even pause to think about what he was going to say. It just came out.

In the van Danny heard the boom. A split second later he was headed for the back door. Two HRT members reached out with over-developed arms and held him back.

"Not yet, Jarhead."

Danny was about to protest but saw the look of determination that he wasn't going anywhere. As fast as the arms went up, they came down. The team was out the back door when they heard Agent Deverse's broadcast and request. There wasn't any mad dash for the front door but a fast, determined walk with the weapons at the low ready. The team entered the building, and the agent on the first floor directed them up to the executive office suite. The trip took less than 30 seconds. Danny trailed along behind. The secretary's office was turned over to the HRT members. The EMTs grabbed the secretary and moved her further away from the action. With the HRT unit covering the door, Deverse backed out of the room with the other plain clothes agents.

"What the hell happened?" Danny asked out of breath.

"The secretary made the call like we planned, and he said he was coming out. But he also told her to get out of the office and that it wasn't her fault. The hair went up on the back of my neck, and I knew something was wrong. The boom came next, and the secretary goes down. I can't figure out how she got hit. Where the hell is the Wiz and his hi-tech shit?"

Chapter 50

The Wiz and two of his techies made their way to the executive office. Each was wearing the torso part of a bomb suit and carried a protective helmet. They lugged a Craftsman tool kit case. With all the gear, the hike up the stairs left them a little winded.

"Whatca got, Obi Wan?"

"Fuck you. I think we have an armed suspect who just shot his secretary is what I think we got."

"As usual you have been misinformed." The Wiz was enjoying the moment. It wasn't often that he saw Deverse in less than 100% control.

"You better start talking fast," said Deverse. "I am running out of patience and ready to strangle someone. You are the closest to me, so you are number one on my list."

"The secretary isn't hit. She didn't take hearing the blast all that well."

"What about the blood? I saw her clothes. She was bleeding all over the place."

"Did you see red?"

"No, I heard her scream and go down. When I turned, she was flopping all around, and her clothes were soaking through with the blood. I had other things to do, and the guys behind me were taking care of her. Before I could check on her, the EMTs got her out of here."

"She is fine," said the Wiz. "Injury wise, that is. She wasn't hit, she just flipped out. The blood, well, she peed in her tighty-whities. No blood. No hit."

"Then I think we have a self-inflicted single gunshot wound to the late Quenton Worthington's body a short distance from here. Would you be so kind as to drill a hole in the door, check for an IED, and find out if our Mr. Worthington is no longer a threat?"

"I would be happy to," said the Wiz. "Okay, guys, let's show 'em why we make the big bucks."

As the bomb team set up their equipment, Agent Deverse had one more thought. "I think I should make at least a token call inside just in case." Of course, there was no answer.

The bomb team took their time and inserted the pinhole camera. There was no need to rush. With the hole finally drilled, the camera was inserted. Everyone crowded around the small TV screen to get a glimpse of what was inside.

"Oh shit," was all the Wiz could say.

"Well?" Deverse wanted to know.

"Unless Mr. Worthington liked the color cranberry red for his main office color, we got ourselves a real mess."

"Can you see him?" Deverse wanted to know.

"There does appear to be someone sitting behind the desk, but there isn't anything from the shoulders up. I think those are shoulders. It is really hard to tell. There is a long gun on the desk pointing at whatever it is sitting behind the desk. I don't see any movement. "

"Keep an eye on things," said Deverse. "Would someone go downstairs and get a card key for the door, so we don't have to drill it."

A voice from the back said, "On the way," and disappeared down the stairs.

A card key was located, and with a quick swipe the door clicked open. Deverse had his gun drawn, but as the door swung open, the gun arm dropped down to his side. Other agents looked over his shoulder. A couple turned away rather quickly before they tossed their cookies.

The office was beautifully appointed and displayed wildlife trophies from around the world. It was more like a museum than an office--or maybe something Teddy Roosevelt might have had. That is except for the back wall. To say the back wall was a mess was an understatement. The desk wasn't much better. Deverse stood in the doorway, and no one moved past him. The shotgun rested on the desk. What was left of the late Quenton Worthington clutched a ruler in his right hand. It looked like he needed to use it to reach the trigger. Everything of the late Quenton Worthington from the neck up was now on full display with an elk and two white tailed deer mounted on the back wall. Even with all the blood and brains, the elk and deer sported very impressive racks. Danny took a quick look over Deverse's shoulder.

"Son of a bitch--a fucking ten gauge," said Danny.

Deverse turned to Danny. "From here you can tell that's a ten gauge?"

"Oh, yeah, that is a ten gauge. That is the same type shotgun that took Penny's head off. But she got hit with a slug. This looks like double 0 buck. If it is a three-inch magnum load, then there could be eighteen double 0 nine-millimeter chunks of lead flying."

In the back an agent who hadn't gotten a look inside asked if they needed an EMT to come up and check for signs of life.

"No, that won't be necessary," said Deverse. "Wiz, it is now your scene. Let me know what you need."

"Two weeks off, Obi Wan."

"Screw you."

"Love ya, too, boss."

Chapter 51

Quenton was dead. Penny was dead. Gary just missed getting killed for peeing in the wrong spot. Brad stuck with his claim that he was nuts. The hot babe of a shrink was still standing beside him. How could all this happen in quiet, beautiful downtown Maidstone? The Feds weren't letting Danny go back on the road, but they also didn't give him anything to do. Danny hated doing nothing fulltime. There were only so many hikes to take. Daytime TV sucked. But Danny hadn't played a major role in the take down. He was there, but after the fact. Yes, it was a ten-gauge shotgun with buck shot. Yes, that was in fact Quenton Worthington sitting at his desk. A lot had been resolved with Quenton's death. But they still did not have a lead on who paid off Detective Lieutenant Snyder. Why had Quenton decided to checkout, especially with a shotgun? With his money and influence, he could have stayed out of jail on bond for who knows how long. Even if he got convicted, there would be the endless appeals. The trucking company was still in operation under a federally appointed receivership management team. But it wasn't like under Quenton. Customers were moving to other vendors. To top it off, it was Danny's fault. First, he wouldn't let a tragic domestic fade away. Then he had to bring down the fixer. Now his meddling brought the federal authorities to Maidstone and gutted the biggest taxpayer/employer in town.

The fact that Danny was right, and he was bringing down flagrant criminals, was beside the point. Then the phone call came.

"Danny, we need to talk." It was Deverse, and he sounded more serious then Danny had ever heard.

"Fine," said Danny, "where and when?"

"Two hours and bring scotch and ice. Make it good scotch, and I will pay you back. Bring Bear with you. See you at York Lake."

"What the hell?" said Danny.

"I will explain. It will take scotch and time, and Bear needs to hear this."

Now this was the strangest thing Danny had ever heard. But Deverse always knew what he was doing so Danny agreed.

"Just how did you decide on York Lake?" Danny wanted to know.

"It is a good place for quiet talk….a place where you can engage in deep reflection and serious thought, don't you think?"

"Yes," and the line went dead.

Danny stopped off in Great Barrington and picked up a bottle of Glen Morgangi. With no rush he made his way to the lake. Agent Deverse wasn't there. Danny walked Bear around and tossed sticks in the lake that Bear dutifully retrieved. The FBI car pulled into the lot, and Agent Deverse exited the vehicle. It was one of the few times Danny had seen Deverse in something other than a suit or at least a sports jacket and tie. Blue jeans, sweatshirt, and sneakers were the uniform of the day. Bear ran over to greet Deverse and was rewarded with a dog cookie. Now Bear had a new best friend and wasn't leaving his side just in case there was a second. From the smell of Deverse's pocket, there was a good chance he

249

would get lucky. This was a lot of firsts for Danny. The three moved to a picnic table and took a seat.

"Where is the scotch?"

Danny produced a Gatorade bottle. This brought a look of disgust to Deverse's normally passive face. "I said scotch, good scotch, and you bring frigin Gatorade?"

"It is scotch, good scotch. The park does not allow the consumption of alcohol, so I transferred it to a sports bottle. Trust me, I am out seventy-five dollars, and I have the receipt."

Deverse wasn't sure. When he took a sip, everything was right with the world.

"It just doesn't seem right to be pouring good scotch from a Gatorade bottle."

"If one of the park rangers came around and saw us with a bottle, he would have to say something. It would be obvious. Chances are if he pays attention, he will know we aren't sharing Gatorade, but he won't care. It's not like we are a bunch of eighteen-year-olds with a case of Bud smashing the bottles in the fireplace. Then again, if he is a prick and busts your balls, you can always pull your FBI creds out and tell him to get lost. Big stakeout or something, you can tell him."

"Got it. I still don't like it, but I got it."

"So why are we here? What do you have to tell me?"

Agent Deverse took a hefty sip in scotch and leaned back against the picnic table. Bear made a move under his right hand and almost sent the scotch flying. Deverse shifted the scotch to his left hand and began to rub Bear's ears. He had a lot to say and was trying to figure out where to start. Danny could see the stress and concentration on Deverse's face and didn't interrupt his train of thought. Finally, after a few more sips, Deverse began to speak.

"Quenton's suicide wasn't because we raided the place and had an arrest warrant. He had been planning to take his own life for weeks, possibly months. Our raid on the place just locked in the date."

"And you know all this because?"

"Quenton had been banging on his computer laying it all out. There are pages and pages of notes and directives about life, his thoughts, and how to keep the trucking company from going under once he was gone."

"Did he give it up that he paid off Snyder?"

"Of all the things he wrote down, that was not one of them. He never even acknowledged that Snyder was paid off. From the sounds of it, he would have been the last person to pay Snyder off to bag the case."

"The last person to spring his son from a murder wrap?"

"The absolute last."

Now Danny was hearing what Deverse was saying, but not understanding. Quenton was the one person with the money and connections to get Brad off. "If not Quenton, then who?"

"Remember the stories that came out about Brad and Penny being swingers? Well, it wasn't swinging. Sex, yes. But not swinging. Do you also remember all those tickets to all the games in and around Boston to get Brad out of town?"

"Yes, of course."

"We found that while he got those tickets from several different people, only one person paid for them, Quenton."

"What?"

"Penny, according to the notes we found on the computer, was Quenton's lover. The night she was killed, Brad caught Quenton at the house naked in bed with Penny. You know the rest of the story."

251

Danny was trying to picture Quenton and Penny together. There had to be a twenty-five-year difference in ages. Quenton was a good-looking guy and had stayed in shape. It had been rumored that he was quite the lady's man, but nothing about Penny being his mistress came out. Now Quenton's wife was about the same age as Quenton and took very good care of herself. They were always seen together around town, but there were trips they each took around the country solo. No one thought anything of it and wrote it off to conflicting schedules.

Deverse went on. "When Penny ended up dead that night, Quenton blamed himself. He almost checked out that day but had to tie up loose ends with the business. Quenton the control freak that he was didn't trust turning over the business to his kids. He was planning on doing himself in a few days after the murder, but he kept finding things to do. Our raid finally gave him no alternative."

"So, who paid Snyder?"

"No idea. Guess where they would meet for lunch and a little afternoon delight."

"I don't know. I would guess someplace out of the way where they wouldn't be seen. Maybe over in New York State."

Agent Deverse sipped his scotch and took a prolonged look around the lake. It was beautiful. You could not see a house or a main road in any direction. Off to the north several geese floated on the water. It was a picture of serenity.

"How about a nice, really quiet secluded lake?"

"No way."

"He loved this place."

"Now I have to find another lake. Son of a bitch!"

"Oh, and one more thing, did you ever figure out why Cornell had such a hard on for you?"

"No, and at this point I don't care."

"You know about the two divorces?"

"Of course."

"But you didn't know that after their divorces, the two ex-wives ran off with Marines."

"That's it. He makes my life miserable because his ex-wives like Marines?"

"That is Part One. Part Two is that neither of the ex-wives would get married, and he had to keep paying alimony."

"Some more scotch please."

Made in the USA
Middletown, DE
25 March 2019